AUTUMN'S QUEST

CHERYL BRAGINSKY

ISBN: 978-0-57847-492-2 (print)
ISBN: 978-0-57847-498-4 (ebook)

TABLE OF CONTENTS

I dedicate this book to my husband Carl, whose faith in me never wavered, and whose copy editing skills were priceless. I am also grateful to my sons, Noel and Tim Tendick, who always stepped up with helpful suggestions and encouraging words when I most needed them. And finally to my friend and critique partner Joli Allen, whose editing expertise and tireless encouragement got me through many difficult and challenging times.

CHAPTER ONE

Rain soaked her wings, branches battered her body, and the raging wind blew her side ways and backward, but Autumn Primrose refused to give up. Even when a cascade of drenching water poured over her face, she kept flying.

A front page story in this morning's Fairy Gazette had warned residents of Golden Wood a massive storm was headed their way. As soon as she read it, Autumn ran to gather coils of rope. She knew high winds from the storm could destroy the grove of saplings she'd planted only yesterday. So she raced to the Dark Forest, determined to tie the young trees to stakes before the storm hit and tore them apart.

Hurrying from tree to tree, she'd barely finished when the storm arrived. Her job done, she took a deep breath. She'd saved the trees, but she couldn't rest yet. She was still deep in the forest with a storm raging all around her. Now she must make her way home.

The tiny fairy, not much bigger than a hummingbird, was almost invisible as she flew through the giant trees of the Dark Forest.

As she battled the wind and rain, a feeling that she was in danger crept into her bones. It wasn't fear of the storm that kept her looking over her shoulder. It was her sense that something she couldn't see followed her in the darkness.

All afternoon she'd had the impression that she was being watched. But whenever she'd looked around, there was nothing to see. Yet her fairy intuition still told her something lurked in the shadows.

As Autumn flew on, she crashed into a massive branch. She grabbed hold of its long pine needles and fought to catch her breath. Weighed down by water-soaked wings, her body numb with cold, she pressed her face against the needles. She longed to cling to the giant tree, but she knew she had to get home to Golden Wood. The Council of Elders met tomorrow and she must be there. So she summoned up her strength and forced herself to let go of the branch.

She decided to fly close to the ground in order to avoid the wind, but the undergrowth still whirled around her. She dodged the waving branches, and pumped her wings harder and harder. Pain flashed through the muscles in her back. All at once a powerful gust of wind caught her off balance and sent her plummeting head over heels toward the flooded ground. Just as she was about to hit a churning current of muddy water, long vines like writhing snakes waved before her eyes. She reached out and clung to them, her last chance to survive.

But the vines weren't there to save her. Thorns as sharp as daggers wove through her hair, and dug into the skin of her arms and legs. The vines wrapped themselves around her like a spider binds a fly, and pulled her close.

She fought to break free of the huge thorn bush that was holding her, but its vines were stronger than she was. Desperate to escape, she looked directly into the center of the bush. Two huge yellow eyes glared back at her. Holy fairy toes! This was no ordinary plant!

The creature tightened its hold as Autumn beat against it with her fists.

"Let me go!"

She yanked at the branches, but thorns pierced her hands. She tried to twist out of its grip, but the creature's hold was too strong.

"You can't escape from me," her captor taunted. It spoke in a hoarse whisper, but the threat came through loud and clear.

It felt like her heart stopped beating. "You're a boggart," she whispered.

As an icy chuckle confirmed her fear as she forced herself to look into the creature's eyes.

"Boggarts are banned from the Fairy Realm," she said, sounding calmer than she felt. "If an elf warrior catches you here you'll be killed."

"I'm not the one that's caught," the boggart sneered.

Holding her so tightly she couldn't move, the boggart set off through the forest. The creature shoved aside plants that got in its way as branches snapped and broke under its heavy feet.

"Where are you taking me?"

The boggart ignored her.

"You can't do this!" she cried. "Don't you know who I am?"

"I know exactly who you are," the evil creature replied. "I recognized you the moment I saw you. That's why I followed you. When I deliver you to my leader, I will be a hero." It gave her an evil smile. "And you will die."

Frightened, Autumn tried to draw back, but there was nowhere to go. The monster's hold was too tight.

The beast trudged on through the wind and rain until at last it stopped to rest. Apparently convinced that its prisoner was under control, it sat down on a fallen log and relaxed its grip. As she felt the vines loosen, Autumn searched for a way to break free. All at once she remembered the yellow eyes. Long, wicked thorns stuck out like swords all around her. In a flash she slid out of the boggart's hold, broke off the longest thorn in sight, aimed at one of the creature's eyes, and stabbed the thorn deep within it. The evil monster howled as Autumn zoomed away.

She flew as fast as she could, desperate to get away before the boggart recovered and came after her. She didn't care which way she went, she just had to escape. When she thought she'd gone far enough, she stopped to get her bearings.

"I like the way you did that," a voice said.

Autumn gasped and whirled around.

A tall elf, dressed in the uniform of a warrior, stood on a branch behind her. He was about five inches tall, an inch taller than Autumn.

"Where did you come from?" she demanded.

"I was on my way through the forest when I heard the commotion that monster made as it crashed through the underbrush. I decided to check it out. I've followed you ever since."

Before she could say anything else, the boggart burst out of the bushes and grabbed her with his thorny vines.

"Got you!" he said, twisting the vines so tight she could barely breathe. "I'll kill you for what you did to me." The eye she had stabbed was dark and bloody. But the other was wide open and glaring at her.

"I don't think so," the elf warrior said.

The boggart's head jerked up, his good eye wide with surprise. Before he could react, the elf warrior landed beside him sword in hand, and slashed the vines that held the helpless fairy. The creature screamed as he dropped his prisoner. Blood spurted everywhere as bits of severed branches fell to the ground. Autumn jumped up from where she'd fallen and ran to hide behind a nearby bush. The elf disappeared.

The shape shifting boggart morphed into a towering figure dressed in a black robe with a hood that hid its face. What remained of its arm hung out of the bloody shreds of a long, dark sleeve. It twisted and turned as it searched for its attacker.

Just then the elf reappeared on the branch of a tree above the boggart. He grabbed a rope of ivy and swung toward the hooded creature. This time his sword was aimed at the boggart's throat.

But before the elf could reach it, the boggart morphed into a snarling tiger and lashed out at the elf warrior with long wicked claws. The elf swung up out of reach, only to drop back down in front of the creature's snarling face. Before the boggart could change shape again, the elf slit its throat. Blood gushed everywhere. The boggart collapsed in a shapeless mass.

After a long moment, Autumn stepped out from behind the bush where she'd been hiding.

"Are you OK?" the elf asked.

"Yes, of course," she said, though her voice shook and she averted her eyes from the body lying in a heap on the ground. She focused on the figure standing before her.

He was about a head taller than she was, dressed all in green, from the slouched hat on his head to his practical boots. He had a bow and a quiver of porcupine quills slung across his back, and his sword sheathed at his side. On his jacket he wore the badge of Blackcedar, lord of the North Woods, a region far away in the northern most part of the realm.

"Thank you for coming to my rescue."

The elf warrior nodded to acknowledge her words, but his face was stern. He appeared to be extremely annoyed.

"I think you'd better tell me what a young fairy like you is doing all alone in the Dark Forest on a night like this."

Autumn frowned. How dare he talk to her as if she was a child! She straightened up to her full height of four inches, and prepared to set him straight. But he wasn't finished.

"You'd best come with me. We'll take shelter in that sycamore tree across the clearing. Then you can explain how you came to be captured by a boggart."

Now Autumn was really mad. She wasn't accustomed to being told what to do. After all, she was no ordinary fairy. But before she could protest, the elf ran across the ground and began to climb the sycamore tree.

She'd crossed her arms, prepared to show him she did not take orders from strange elves even if they were elf warriors, when she realized she was all alone on the forest floor. Rain was pelting down on her head, she was getting wetter and colder by the moment, and she suddenly realized there could be other boggarts lurking nearby. So she decided to join the elf warrior in the sycamore tree. But she did not intend to let him get way with giving her orders.

CHAPTER TWO

"**N**ow tell me, what you are doing all alone at night deep in the Dark Forest in the middle of a massive storm?" the elf warrior demanded as Autumn settled down on the branch beside him.

"Do you know who I am?" she asked, ignoring his question.

"No." The elf warrior frowned. He wasn't accustomed to being disobeyed.

"I'm Autumn Primrose."

"Oh." He looked at her without speaking for a moment. Then he removed his hat, and nodded his head in her direction. "It's an honor to meet you, Your Highness."

That said, he resumed his interrogation, apparently unimpressed at meeting the future queen of the Fairy Realm.

"Elf warriors are responsible for guarding the realm," he told her. "As an elf warrior, I've sworn to protect the folk and creatures that live here, including you. So I need to know what you are doing all alone in the forest. You should have had guards to protect you. No wonder you were kidnapped by a boggart. Don't you understand that creature would have turned you over to your enemies? "

Autumn stiffened. She did *not* like being lectured. After all, she was a princess. But she was also confused. She didn't have any enemies. What in the Realm was he so upset about?

"I'm a tree healer," she told him. "I always come to the forest alone. It's my job. And I have no idea what you're talking about. Azara and her boggarts were my only enemies, and they were banished from the Realm years ago. So now it's your turn to answer a question. How in the realm did that boggart get here?

"That's just it. Azara escaped from prison. She and her army of boggarts are back. Your enemies have returned. "

For a moment Autumn simply stared at him in shocked silence. "I don't believe you. Azara's prison is on the top of Ice Mountain. She's guarded night and day. She couldn't possibly escape."

"But she has," he replied. "Her army of boggarts broke in, killed the elves that guarded her, and set her free. Then they all disappeared. Except for the one that just tried to kidnap you, that is."

He looked at her for a long moment.

"So that's why he kidnapped you," he said at last. "I get it now. What a prize you would have been to take to Azara! With you dead, it would be much easier for her to regain the throne."

"What do you mean regain the throne? Autumn protested in alarm. "She can't do that! The entire realm rebelled against her. When she was defeated, she was sentenced to spend the rest of her life in prison, and her entire boggart army was banished forever!"

"The problem was, she never accepted her defeat," He replied. "Ever since she was sent to prison, she's been plotting to return. Why do you think she sent for her boggart army? She's just been waiting for the Realm to let down its defenses. It seems she's decided the time has come."

"I don't understand," Autumn replied in a shaken voice.

She took a deep breath and struggled to regain her composure. When she spoke again, her voice was firm.

"Why should I believe you?" she asked, crossing her arms. "Who are you? And how do you know all this about Azara?"

"I'm Captain Lanceleaf Cottonwood. I was with Lord Blackcedar when it was discovered Azara had escaped. Now I've been sent to warn the rest of the realm. I was on my way to see your grandmother, Queen Rose, and Lord Redcedar when I came upon you and the boggart."

"If what you're telling me is true, we'd better warn them immediately." Autumn shook out her wings and prepared to take flight.

"Hold on a moment. I think it would be better to wait until morning. We're still a long way from Golden Wood and the storm is worse than ever. You're tired, your clothes are soaked, and so are your wings. There aren't many hours of night left. It would be better to rest and start fresh in the morning."

Autumn frowned. She'd never expected Azara to return. She was angry… and she was scared…and she wanted to get home as fast as she could. But when she thought about the elf warrior's words, she decided he was right.

"Get some sleep," he told her. "I promise you, we'll leave at dawn."

"All right," she agreed. "Dawn it is."

With that the elf warrior climbed to a place higher in the tree to keep watch, while she pulled a cloak from a sack at her waist, wrapped herself in it, and curled up against the trunk of the tree. She fell asleep at once.

CHAPTER THREE

The storm had moved on when Autumn woke up. With the elf warrior on guard, the exhausted fairy had slept soundly through the night. She rubbed her eyes and peered out through the branches of the sycamore. In the early morning light, water dripped steadily from nearby trees and a ghostly mist rose from the ground.

Autumn's gaze was wary as she looked at the forest that surrounded her. Massive trees towered above her, disappearing into the treetop canopy. Laurel bushes and sword ferns rose from the ground and blended into the shadows. They created a wall even fairy eyes couldn't see through. Was that a bush that moved below, or was it a boggart? The light was so dim on the forest floor she couldn't tell. She stood, rolled up her cloak, slipped it into the lily leaf sack at her waist, and shook out her wings.

"Good morning," a voice said from somewhere in the tree above her.

Autumn spun around and looked up. The broad leaves and thick branches of the sycamore tree filled the space overhead like an umbrella. It took a moment for her to spot the elf warrior perched high above her. At the same time, she realized that the forest was unusually quiet. No bird calls broke the stillness. No flurry of squirrel feet scampered up the trees.

"Come on up to the top of the tree," He called down to her. "The sun will be up soon."

Autumn fluttered toward the treetop her mind awhirl with questions. *Where is Azara? Where is her boggart army? Are they hiding in the shadows? What happened to the forest creatures?*

When she arrived at the top, the sun was beginning to bathe it with light. She settled on the branch beside the elf warrior.

"Where is everyone?" she asked. "I haven't seen or heard a single creature since I woke up." Her voice tightened. "Have you seen any sign of Azara or her boggarts?

"A few boggarts passed through here during the night," the elf warrior told her. "That's why the forest creatures have fled. Azara was every bit as cruel to the animals as she was to the fairies."

"The Council of Elders meets this morning," Autumn said after a moment. She spoke in the most composed voice she could muster. She was badly frightened, not for herself, but for her grandmother.

After Azara's defeat, before the Realm's evil queen was led away to prison, she had vowed to return and kill Rose. Rose had led the rebellion after Azara killed Autumn's parents, the uprising's original leaders.

"Folk from throughout the realm will attend this meeting," Autumn went on. "The gallery will be packed with fairies, elves, pixies, and gnomes. It would be an ideal place for you to spread the word of Azara's return." She paused. "Of course, it would also be the perfect time for a surprise attack. Do you think that's her plan?" she asked as she shot the elf a worried look.

"No one knows what she's planning," Captain Cottonwood replied. "She escaped two days ago. She hasn't been seen since."

Autumn jumped up.

"You said we'd leave at dawn. It's time to go!"

She took off flying as fast as she could through the forest. The elf warrior followed, easily keeping up with her though he ran below her on the forest floor. As she flew, she glanced upward again and again. If only she could spot a hawk or a raven. A bird would carry them much faster than they could travel on their own. But there was still no sign of any of the woodland creatures.

The two of them kept up their rapid pace until at last they emerged from the forest's shadowy darkness. As they stood on the top of a hill, the orchards of Golden Wood lay before them. Row upon row of leafy green trees spread out in every direction. Bright orange poppies and wild blue iris blanketed the ground. The storm had moved on, and the sun shone bright in a blue sky.

Here the trees were full of birds, their chatter a burst of noise after the ominous silence of the forest. Autumn landed beside the elf warrior while they stopped to catch their breath.

"You need to go straight to Lord Redcedar," she said, sounding like the princess she was. "He's responsible for the defense of Golden Wood. He needs to know what's happened as soon as possible. I'll explain the situation to my grandmother."

"Are you sure you don't want me to come with you?" He was torn between his duty to guard the future queen and the need to warn Lord Redcedar.

"I'll be safe now. After all I'm almost home. There are plenty of folk here to help me if I need them."

He knew she was right, but he couldn't stop himself from giving her one final warning.

"You do understand you're in great danger?"

"Of course I do, Captain Cottonwood. But if you think I'm going to let Azara frighten me, you'd better think again. Now go!" She stood up straight, held her head high, and stuck out her chin. She was ready to stand up to anybody. The elf warrior smiled slightly and left.

CHAPTER FOUR

After the dark of the forest, Golden Wood felt warm and peaceful. It was harvest time and row after row of trees were filled with oranges, plums, apples, and cherries. But it wasn't just ripe fruit that filled the trees with color. The orchards also overflowed with a dozen shades of fairy cottages, from periwinkle blue to lemon yellow.

The fairy houses were built of twigs and branches woven into every shape imaginable. They were decorated with nuts, pebbles, feathers, and a vast array of colorful flowers. A host of bluebirds, robins, and tiny yellow finches brightened the orchards even more. It looked as if a rainbow had been woven through the trees.

Yet, even amongst the color and light, Autumn knew there were dark shadows.

Huge heaps of blackened waste from Azara's abandoned mines were scattered among the beautiful trees. Rotten and sulfurous, they gave off a smell that sickened Autumn as she flew above them.

In some places, once productive orchards lay waste, the trees cut down and burned for fuel in Azara's factories. But while these areas of devastation were ugly, Autumn knew that what the wicked queen had done to the folk of Golden Wood was even worse.

Azara had used them as slaves to work in her mines. She'd imprisoned them far below ground where many were killed by Azara's boggarts. Others were victims of the poisoned air and toxic water. Even more suffered the heartbreak of being imprisoned far from their families and the world they loved. As Autumn flew on, her determination grew. Azara must never be allowed to return!

Below her she saw several farmers already working in their fields, including Farmer Bunchberry. Dressed in an outfit of cotton overalls, plaid shirt, and practical boots, he was shepherding his flock of ladybug beetles toward a nearby rose garden. He didn't look like one of the most respected leaders of the Fairy Realm, but he was. Not only was he a member of the Council of Elders, he was her grandmother's oldest friend and chief advisor.

Autumn longed to stop and talk to him now, to ask his advice on how to break the news to Gran. But she knew she didn't have time so she flew on. She would have to tell her grandmother as best she could

At last she arrived at Rose's cottage in a mulberry tree. Window boxes of tiny white flowers glowed against its mellow walls. Smoke from the morning fire swirled out of the chimney that rose from the thatched roof. *How am I going to do this?* Autumn thought as she landed on a branch by her grandmother's front door. *How can I tell her Azara's back?*

While Autumn was trying to summon up the words, Rose flung the door open. "Welcome home!" she cried as she gave Autumn a grandmotherly hug.

Both Rose and Autumn were small, even for fairies. They both had large, dark eyes, and pointed ears that stood straight up like thorns. Autumn let her long, dark hair hang down her back, while her grandmother piled her gray hair on top of her head, but otherwise the two were very much alike.

"Oh my dear," Rose said, standing back and looking Autumn over. "What's happened to you? You've got scrapes and bruises everywhere."

"I'm all right, Gran," Autumn said, putting her arm around her grandmother. "But I've got something to tell you. Let's go inside." Autumn led her grandmother into the parlor. Now that the time had come, she still had no idea how to break the news. She knew it would stir up painful emotions from the past, so she didn't want to just blurt it out.

"Gran, would you like a cup of tea?"

Now Rose began to look worried. "I always know when you're upset about something, Autumn. Tell me what's wrong."

Autumn took a deep breath and looked her grandmother in the eye.

"It's Azara, Gran. She's escaped from prison. And her boggarts are back too. One of them tried to kidnap me last night. Lord Blackcedar thinks Azara intends to try to retake the throne."

Rose's pink cheeks turned pale, and her dark eyes got even darker. She sat absolutely still for a long moment before she reached out and grasped Autumn's hand.

"Tell me."

Autumn repeated everything she'd learned from the elf warrior, and then added the story of the events of the night before.

"I don't understand how this could happen." Rose sat and stared before her as if looking at something far away. At last she got to her feet.

"Come Autumn. I'll put something on those wounds." She didn't mention Azara and Autumn knew her grandmother well enough to know there was nothing more to be said.

Rose spread a healing salve made from comfrey leaves on Autumn's scrapes and bruises. "You were just a baby when we drove Azara and her boggarts from the Realm," she said when she'd finished. "You don't know how evil they are. Azara and that boggart would have killed you." She gave Autumn a long, hard hug. "I'm so grateful you're all right." There were tears in her eyes but she forced a smile and told Autumn to go and get ready. It was almost time for the council meeting.

Autumn dashed into her bedroom. She glanced longingly at her bird's nest bed, but there was no time to rest. She washed her face in the walnut shell basin, put on her favorite orange poppy-colored dress, added a pair of yellow stockings, and used a thistle to comb her hair.

As she was about to go out the door, she hesitated… then walked to her nest and reached beneath her pillow. She pulled out a worn gossamer scarf and, burying her face in it, whispered a single word… *Mama*…then she took a shaky breath. She held the scarf against her face a moment more then put it away and hurried to the kitchen. She ate a blueberry and a slice of poppy seed bread then joined her grandmother at the door. As they started to leave, Autumn paused in the doorway.

"Gran, I don't understand this. How can Azara be so evil? She's your brother's only child… she's part of our family."

Her grandmother hesitated, and then looked Autumn in the eye.

"I don't know… at least not for sure…And I probably shouldn't say this…because there's no way to prove it…but there used to be stories…" Rose took a breath and a rush of words spilled out.

"Azara's mother died not long after Azara was born. Zelda was incredibly beautiful, but she was cold. And she could be cruel. The fairy folk had wondered about her from the beginning, for the way the king met her was strange.

"Most visitors from distant places came to see the king with a formal entourage and a great deal of ceremony. Zelda simply turned up at court one day. She claimed to be a princess from the distant north and had an odd group of folk travelling with her. Her companions rarely spoke to anyone and stayed in the woods outside of the town.

"Leopold fell in love with her at first sight and married her within the week. Because no one knew who she was or where she came from, it isn't surprising there were rumors about her past. But the story that came to be told was alarming. It was said she was a shape shifter, a boggart, who had taken the form of a beautiful fairy princess to captivate the king.

"Leopold didn't believe what folk said. He said the courtiers were just jealous of her beauty. Still, the rumors persisted…and I've always thought that if they were true and Zelda was a boggart… it would explain a lot."

"Like what?"

"Like Azara's boggart army and her overwhelming greed for power and wealth. Boggarts are known for their love of jewels, of gold, and precious stones. If Azara is half boggart it explains her obsession with the mines and the wicked way she forced the fairy folk to work in them."

"Do you think its true then? Do you think Azara could be part boggart?"

"I don't know, Autumn. I don't think anyone will ever know for sure. Both her parents are dead. But I have my suspicions. Anyway, it doesn't really matter. It's what happens now that's important."

"What do you think she'll do now that she's free?" Autumn asked. She tried to sound matter-of-fact, but her voice wavered a little at the end.

"I have no idea."

CHAPTER FIVE

Golden Wood's Council of Elders met in a vast cavern, its entrance hidden in the roots of a towering oak tree. Although the chamber was underground, it was anything but dark. Lit by lanterns placed high on the walls, it was a constantly moving dance of light and shadow.

Bleachers filled with hundreds of elves, fairies, pixies, and gnomes lined the lofty walls, all the way from the dirt floor to a ceiling of woven tree roots. Fairies dressed in bright colors laughed, chatted, and constantly fluttered about. They looked like a mass of colorful flowers waving in the breeze.

A walnut table, honed by the skillful hands of elvish craftsmen, sat in the exact center of the floor. Along one side of the table, four chairs made of hemlock twigs provided seating for the Council.

Lord Redcedar, Farmer Bunchberry, and Calypso, leader of the pixies, were already seated when Rose and Autumn arrived. Queen

Rose took her place at the center of the table, while Autumn went to sit by her best friend Violet, in the gallery's front row.

"It's not like you to be late," Violet said. "Is anything wrong?"

"I spent the night in the Dark Forest," Autumn replied. "I didn't get home until this morning."

"You were alone all night in the Dark Forest! I don't believe it! You've got to be the only fairy I know who wouldn't be terrified."

"I'd be a pretty useless tree healer if I was afraid to spend the night in the forest," she said with a smile. She was amused by her friend's alarm. Although they were best friends, they were as different as two fairies could be.

"Anyway, there was more going on last night than just the storm." She quickly told her friend about being kidnapped by the boggart, and how she was rescued, but she didn't mention Azara. Somehow she couldn't bring herself to say that hated name.

Violet's eyes were huge by the time Autumn finished. Although she'd been a witness to Autumn's escapades ever since they were tiny, she'd never heard a story like this.

"Gracious goblins, Autumn!" she said. "How can you be so calm? If that had happened to me, I'd still be shaking! But tell me more about the elf warrior. He sounds awfully brave. Is he handsome?"

"You can decide that for yourself. He'll be here any minute."

It was time for the meeting to begin. The gallery settled down and all eyes focused on Lord Redcedar. The elf lord was tall, with a carefully trimmed beard and dark eyes under even darker eyebrows.

He wore black boots, a black suit, and a red cloak. He stood beside the Council table to Rose's right, ready to call the meeting to order.

Farmer Bunchberry, still dressed in the work clothes he had worn when Autumn saw him earlier on his farm, was seated on her left. Calypso, the leader of the pixies, sat next to him. Like most of his folk, the pixie was dressed all in brown, his clothing matched by brown hair and eyes. It was easy to see why pixies made such excellent spies. They were perfectly camouflaged. Only Calypso's twinkling eyes and ready smile stood out, giving him a merry look, a fact which had always made him a favorite of Autumn's.

Autumn was still searching the hall for Captain Cottonwood, when Lord Redcedar rapped on the table. As the overlord of Golden Wood, he would conduct the meeting, but it was Queen Rose who had the final authority when it came to making decisions.

"Good morning, Your Majesty," Lord Redcedar said, turning to Rose with a slight bow. "And good morning Your Highness," he said with a respectful nod to Autumn. "Greetings Council members and good day to all of you gathered in the gallery.

"The original purpose of this meeting was to discuss preparations for winter. But I've just learned that a far greater danger than winter faces our land. "

The members of the audience glanced at each other. No one made a sound.

"I want to introduce Captain Lanceleaf Cottonwood. He brings a message from my cousin, Lord Blackcedar of the Great North Wood. Please give him your complete attention."

The elf warrior strode forward from the back of the chamber.

Autumn watched his arrival wondering what he would say. She knew the news was going to be a huge shock.

As if he knew what she was thinking, the elf's eyes met hers as he took his place before the Council. He stood there, straight and tall, his face grave. He was a commanding figure. For many it was the first time they'd ever seen an elf warrior this close.

No one made a sound except Violet, who whispered "Wow!" in Autumn's ear.

Autumn smiled briefly at her friend, though worry lines remained between her eyes. Her hands were clenched as she leaned forward to hear what the elf would say.

"I bring a message from Lord Blackcedar to the folk of Golden Wood," Lance announced in a voice that carried to the highest balcony. "Azara, former queen of the Fairy Realm, has escaped from her prison on Ice Mountain. Her army of boggarts has returned as well."

The room exploded with sound as everyone began talking at once. Violet grabbed Autumn's arm.

"Why didn't you tell me?"

"I didn't know what to say. I can hardly believe it myself."

A nervous, twittering fairy named Philomena was sitting nearby. She fluttered up and down, her hand over her heart, her eyes flickering around the room as she uttered little squeaks of alarm. Suddenly she focused on Autumn.

"It's all your parents' fault," she scolded. "Hawk and Marigold never should have encouraged the rebellion. They should have left well enough alone."

For a moment Autumn sat absolutely still, frozen as if turned to ice.

Autumn's parents had died because folk throughout the realm begged them to lead a rebellion against Azara. They'd agreed because they knew it was the only way to stop the suffering and devastation caused by the evil queen. But Azara and her boggarts killed them when the rebellion was just beginning. It was Rose who'd led the battle that drove Azara from the throne.

Autumn's icy calm erupted into a blazing flame of anger.

"Are you saying they should have ignored the pleas of the fairy folk and left them to die?" Autumn demanded. Her voice shook as she stood to face Philomena.

Philomena ignored her words and fluttered away, determined to sit as far from Autumn as possible.

Violet put her arm around her friend. "Don't pay any attention to her. If it weren't for your parents and your grandmother, the folk of the realm would still be Azara's slaves."

Autumn was still angry, but she sat back down as Lord Redcedar pounded on the table to quiet the room.

"Let Captain Cottonwood finish."

"Lord Blackcedar believes Azara will attempt to regain the throne," Lance said. "She must be recaptured. He is asking Queen Rose to hold a council of war immediately."

High in the back of the gallery a voice rang out. "We don't need any more wars. If Azara wants to come back, I say we let her. Why should more fairy folk die?"

All eyes turned to the speaker, a large gnome, dressed all in grey, with a hat that cast a shadow over his face.

In response to his words, one or two voices called out "Hear, hear." But among the rest of the folk silence hung like a thick fog. Then they all began to shout at once.

"What are you saying, you fool?" an elf in the middle balcony shouted. "Have you forgotten all the folk who died in Azara's mines?"

"That's right," another elf joined in. "We'll never let those evil creatures return!"

By now everyone in the crowd was on their feet. They shouted at the unknown gnome. "We'll never be her slaves again!"

"You'll be sorry," the gnome replied. With that he stood up and flung off his cloak and hat. Before their eyes, he morphed into a crow. Black feathers covered its body, and wings grew out of its back. He rose up above the crowd and flew toward the top of the cavern.

Suddenly a dagger sliced through the air. With a screech the great bird plummeted toward the ground, a long, slender knife sticking out from its chest. As it fell, it changed its shape once more, becoming a pale, grey-skinned creature that was dead before it hit the ground. It lay there unmoving and almost invisible.

A shocked silence followed as all eyes turned to the dagger's source. A resounding cheer broke out as the fairy folk realized the elf warrior had just killed a boggart.

"I don't believe it," Violet said to Autumn, in a hushed voice. "Where did that horrid thing come from? The way your elf warrior killed it was amazing."

"He isn't my elf warrior," Autumn said, her eyes on Lance. "But he is amazing."

Rose got to her feet. She held up her hand, and immediately the crowd grew quiet.

"Thank you, Captain Cottonwood. Now that we've all seen the danger with our own eyes, I shall call for representatives from every province in the realm to meet in the Gathering Grove by sundown tomorrow. We must devise a plan to drive Azara and her boggarts from the Fairy Realm forever. In the meantime, I ask you all to remain calm. We've defeated Azara in the past. We can do it again."

With that she left the chamber followed closely by Lord Redcedar, Lance, and the rest of the Council. Autumn, too, jumped up and flew toward the exit, with Violet close behind.

"What will happen now?" Violet asked when she and Autumn arrived outside.

"I have no idea," Autumn replied as she prepared to follow her grandmother.

CHAPTER SIX

Autumn flew straight to the citadel high on the hillside across the glen. Pointed turrets and an enormous watchtower guarded the entrance to the stone fortress. This was the home of Lord Redcedar and the headquarters of Golden Wood's army.

Armed with bows and arrows, swords, and crossbows, the guards turned back everyone who approached. A mighty raven brayed out the news of Azara's return from the top of the watchtower. The harsh cry would echo over great distances as the news was relayed from raven to raven throughout the land.

When Autumn landed before the entrance, the guards snapped to attention and saluted, a dramatic contrast to the casual "Good morning, Your Highness" that usually greeted her.

She acknowledged the salute with a nod of her head and passed through the massive doors. An empty courtyard stretched out before her. It was usually an active market place overflowing with fairy folk, but today there was no one in sight.

Autumn hurried across the vacant square and entered a vast central hall. Ancient swords and shields lined the walls of the hall, souvenirs of battles dating from the troll wars of ancient times to the rebellion against Azara. As she walked past the display of weapons, Autumn realized that after her experience in the forest, she had a new understanding of what it a sword fight was like.

But there was more to see than just an array of weapons. On her way across the enormous room, Autumn saw Lord Redcedar, Calypso and several Army officers gathered in the center of the hall. Seated at a large, round table, they were already discussing preparations for war. A line of messenger birds stood at attention behind them, waiting to carry dispatches to all parts of the realm.

Autumn spotted Rose and Farmer Bunchberry sitting in a distant corner. She could tell they were having a heated discussion by the way Farmer Bunchberry puffed on his pipe and Rose shook her head.

"Gran, what will happen now?" Autumn asked, as she landed on a chair beside her grandmother.

"We were just talking about that," Rose said. "Before I leave for the Gathering I want to make sure you understand your position. As heir to the throne, you are the main obstacle to Azara's return. You will be in great danger until we capture her and her boggarts.

You must stay here in Golden Wood where we can protect you until Azara is defeated."

"Oh no!" Autumn exclaimed. "I'm not sitting this out! I intend to be part of this battle. As the future queen, it is my responsibility to help deal with this threat to the realm just as you and my parents did."

"There you see," Farmer Bunchberry put in, looking at Rose. "That's what I was trying to tell you. I understand your desire to protect her, but Autumn has a role to play, and the time has come for her to play it."

The wise old farmer turned to Autumn.

"Your grandmother has taught you to be a healer. The time has come for you to learn to be a warrior."

"I'm ready to ..." Autumn began when her grandmother stood up and put her hands on her hips.

"I've taught Autumn to be a fair, just and compassionate ruler! That's all she needs to know!"

Farmer Bunchberry faced her. He looked just as determined.

"Now, Rose," he said. "We both know you can't always rule by talking things over. Sometimes it's necessary to stand up and fight. Her parents were willing to confront Azara, and so were you. Now it is up to Autumn. It's time to tell her about the Golden Tree."

"Bunchberry, you are my oldest friend, and my most trusted advisor, but it is not your place to discuss the golden tree. That is a subject that concerns the royal family alone."

"What golden tree?" Autumn interrupted. "What are you talking about?"

"I was waiting to tell you the story when you assumed the throne," Rose replied. "A pilgrimage to the golden tree takes place just before every new ruler is crowned. The tree's existence is supposed to be known to the rulers of the realm alone," she added with a meaningful glance at Farmer Bunchberry.

"Don't be so uppity, Rose," the old farmer retorted. "It was you who told me about the power of the tree in the first place... AND you told me how important it was in your own defeat of Azara. Now Azara has to be defeated again and this time it is Autumn who must confront her. It's time for Autumn to go to the Land of the Sea Elves."

Rose stood rigid, hands on hips, confronting her old friend. "It's too soon for her to take on the responsibilities of being queen. There's still time before she comes of age. I don't want her in this fight." Her voice, so strong when she began to talk, sounded almost pleading when she finished.

"She's in it whether you like it or not," he replied. His voice was firm, but his eyes were full of compassion.

"I know how much you have suffered," he told her. "It broke your heart when Azara killed Marigold and Hawk. But if you don't want their deaths to be in vain, we must get rid of Azara once and for all. Our army can deal with Azara's boggarts, but only Autumn can confront Azara."

A series of conflicting emotions passed across Rose's face. The last was resignation. Farmer Bunchberry's face softened as he watched her.

Autumn leaned forward and looked her grandmother in the eye. "I'm no longer a child, Gran. You've got to stop protecting me."

Rose sighed then began to speak.

"The golden tree stands in a hidden grotto in the Land of the Sea Elves. It is a source of a magical power that has been used by the rulers of the Fairy Realm since the beginning of fairy time. It requires determination to make it work, but if you have the courage to use it, it will help you in ways you can't even imagine."

"What kind of ways? What does it do?"

"It enhances your strength, not just of body, but also of mind. The way you use the power it gives depends on you. It can heal, or it can destroy. Azara used it to make slaves of her subjects.

"The tree is guarded by a wood sprite. If she believes you are ready, she will give you a branch. That branch will be yours to use as you wish." Rose looked into Autumn's eyes.

"You've shown that you have courage, my dear," she told her granddaughter. "Now you must use that courage to fulfill your destiny. I'm afraid I can't go with you to get the branch. I must cross the river as soon as possible if I am to reach the Gathering Grove in time. Lord Chiton will tell you how to find the tree when you get to the Land of the Sea Elves. But first we must figure out how to get you there."

"Perhaps I could be of help," said a voice from the shadows behind them.

All three turned to see Captain Cottonwood approach.

"I, too, must go to the Land of the Sea Elves," the elf warrior told them. "Lord Blackcedar ordered me to go there after I delivered the message to Golden Wood. As I waited here to tell you, I couldn't help overhearing what you said. If you want me to, I could accompany you as far as the river, and then go on with Princess Autumn to the sea elves."

Farmer Bunchberry spoke up before Rose could respond. "I think that's a capital idea. What could be safer than to travel with an elf warrior? He's already proven he can protect her."

He turned to face Autumn. "This time has come sooner than we planned, but I believe that you, like your grandmother, can step up when you are needed.

"After your parents were killed, your grandmother took their place as leader of the rebellion. When the rebellion succeeded, and Azara was banished, you became next in line for the throne. But you were too young to rule, so your grandmother has served as queen. Now it is your time to face Azara. But first you must become a warrior. To do that you will need a golden branch."

Just then Lord Redcedar approached. "Your Majesty," he said to Rose. "We must go if we are to arrive at the Gathering Grove in time."

"Yes, of course."

Rose turned to Farmer Bunchberry.

"Take care of Golden Wood, my friend," Rose told him, putting her hand on his shoulder. "You're in charge until we return." She turned and headed toward the door.

Autumn went up to the old farmer and spoke so quietly no one else could hear.

"Do you believe I'm ready to do this?"

"Yes, my dear, I do."

Autumn smiled, gave him a quick hug, and followed her grandmother.

As Queen Rose, Lord Redcedar, Autumn, and Captain Cottonwood made their way across the great hall, Lord Redcedar signaled for six elf warriors to join them. They would escort Rose and Redcedar to the Gathering Grove. Autumn and Lance would travel to the land of the sea elves on their own.

The small party left the citadel in silence.

CHAPTER SEVEN

The travelers made their way along a narrow dirt path as the golden light of afternoon beamed down through the branches of towering evergreen trees. Birds moved restlessly in the canopy high above. Word of the events at the Council had already spread, and the woodland creatures were uneasy. They knew what a fairy war meant. Many of them would serve the realm as spies, messengers, scouts, and even warriors. They, too, could die in battle.

The little group kept a careful lookout as they travelled. Lance, Lord Redcedar, and the elf warriors searched the path ahead and behind, while Queen Rose and Autumn used their farseeing fairy eyes to keep watch on the tree canopy overhead. Autumn tried to stay calm, but memories of her encounter with the boggart flashed in her mind.

As they journeyed deeper into the forest, they increased their pace. There was no time to lose if Queen Rose and Lord Redcedar were to reach the other side of the river before nightfall. No one wanted to be out on the water in the dark.

At last they arrived at the river bank. The river's vast expanse reflected the soft light of late afternoon. The water flowed slowly, the waves in no hurry to make their way to the sea.

"Everything looks so peaceful, Gran," Autumn said. "It's hard to believe the danger is real."

"That boggart at the Council meeting was real enough," her grandmother replied. "So was the one that kidnapped you. You've got to keep your guard up every moment. Until Azara is captured, we are all in danger."

"Hurry!" Lord Redcedar called out from his place farther up the line. "We must cross before dark."

The escort of elves rushed to the river bank. Shoving aside cattails and tule grass, they searched for the hollow cedar bark canoe the local fairy folk used to cross the vast expanse of water.

The elves soon found the slender craft and pulled it from the rushes. They hoisted it up on their shoulders and ran across the sandy beach to the river's edge. There they lowered the canoe into the water and looked cautiously about as they waited to get started.

Lord Redcedar turned to Autumn and Captain Cottonwood.

"Queen Rose and I will cross the river here. We should arrive at the Gathering Grove by nightfall. You two will take the path through the forest to the Land of the Sea Elves. I know I don't have to warn you to be careful."

Rose gave Autumn a final hug. She looked anxious as she held Autumn tight.

"Don't worry, Gran," Autumn said, gently pushing her grandmother back so she could look into her eyes. "I can do this."

But it wasn't easy for Rose to let go. She'd spent too many years trying to keep Autumn safe. Somewhere in the back of her mind, the granddaughter she loved so much was still a little girl.

"Take care of her," she told Lance.

"I will, your Majesty," Lance replied.

Autumn rolled her eyes at her grandmother's words. But her expression was just as worried when she watched Rose climb into the boat.

With four elf warriors in front, Queen Rose and Lord Redcedar in the middle, and two more elves behind, the narrow craft entered the gently flowing river. The water was tranquil as they headed out.

All at once the boat began to rock. The elves peered over the sides, trying to see the cause of the turbulence. Violent currents swirled around them and they struggled to row through the churning water. They dug the paddles in deep, fighting to move ahead. Rose and Redcedar gripped the sides of the boat as the elves wrestled for control.

Horrified, Captain Cottonwood and Autumn watched from the shore. The elf warrior ran forward to help, but the boat was already in deep water.

"Turn back!" Autumn cried out.

But it was too late. The noise of the roiling water drowned out her cry as the river spun the canoe around like a leaf in a whirlpool. There was nothing Autumn and Captain Cottonwood could do but watch.

As the canoe swung about, a gigantic wave rose beside it. The wave towered above the small boat like a dark, forbidding wall. A dozen black-robed creatures loomed inside the wave, mighty shadows with scowling faces. Boggarts!

For an instant everyone in the boat sat frozen with shock. Then the four elf warriors in front drew their swords. Furiously they struck out, slashing and stabbing as they thrust their swords into the wall of boggarts. At the same time, the two elves in the rear of the boat took aim with bows and arrows. They shot arrow after arrow into the boggart line, but the rolling of the boat sent many flying wide of their mark.

The boggarts fought back with swords of their own. They lunged toward the elves in the boat, only to pull back as more and more arrows poured into their ranks. To Autumn and Captain Cottonwood, it was like watching a vortex.

Rose and Lord Redcedar took refuge in the bottom of the boat. The elf lord crouched beside Rose, shielding her with his body, his sword ready to protect her if a boggart came near.

Autumn moved as if to take flight, but drew back. Unarmed, and inexperienced in the ways of fighting, she would only get in the way.

The boggarts increased their efforts, generating more and more turmoil in the water. Suddenly the wave smashed into the canoe, flipped it over and toppled the passengers into the river.

Then the wall of boggarts changed shape, morphing from a huge wave to a giant pair of hands. They grabbed Queen Rose, turned and moved upriver like a backwards tide. Before Lance and Autumn could take it in, they'd vanished from sight, leaving flailing elves in the water, and mocking laughter in their wake.

"Gran!" Autumn screamed. She started to fly after them, but Lance held her back.

"You can't follow them."

Autumn turned to face him. Her expression was frantic.

"I've got to follow them. They're taking my grandmother!"

"Please, your Highness. You can't go after them. They're moving too fast, and we don't know what else might be waiting up there. It's too dangerous. We can't go alone. Besides, they've already vanished."

Autumn looked up river. It was true. No sign of the boggarts remained, not even on the horizon. "But we can't just let them disappear. We've got to follow them."

"The birds will follow them."

As a soldier, Lance knew nothing would be accomplished by racing upriver now, but he recognized Autumn's desperate fear for her grandmother. He hesitated. None of his previous experience had taught him how to handle a desperately upset princess.

Just then Lord Redcedar and the elf warriors staggered to shore from the overturned boat. Cold and exhausted, the elves collapsed onto the beach. Autumn and Lance ran to Lord Redcedar.

"Did you see which way they went?"the elf lord asked.

"They've gone upriver," Captain Cottonwood replied. "They're already out of sight."

"That's what I feared."

"We must follow them," Autumn said. "We must rescue Gran." Unconsciously she tugged on Lord Redcedar's arm as if to pull him upriver.

Lord Redcedar firmly disengaged her hand from his arm.

"I'm sorry, Princess Autumn; I know this is hard for you. But nothing would be accomplished if we followed them now."

Autumn looked frantically from Lord Redcedar to Captain Cottonwood.

"If we want to save Queen Rose, we've got to get help," the elf warrior told her.

"I agree," Lord Redcedar said. "Autumn, you and Captain Cottonwood must continue on your way to the sea elves. They are better prepared for battle on the river. They will help you rescue your grandmother. Meanwhile I will continue to the Gathering Place. We must speed up our preparations. It is clear Azara and her boggarts could attack at any time. The two of you must travel as fast as you can. But remember, Azara and her boggarts could be anywhere."

Autumn took one last look upriver, before she turned and followed the elf warrior. Her face was troubled as they started down the trail to the sea. All at once she called out for him to stop. She folded her arms across her chest, and regarded him steadily.

"I don't understand this," she said. "My grandmother's life is at stake and Lord Redcedar is leaving it up to a single elf warrior, an unarmed princess who has no idea how to fight, and a few sea elves to rescue her? Wouldn't it be better for us to return and gather the entire Golden Wood army? Surely they would be able to mount a better rescue mission."

The elf tried to explain. "After what just happened, Lord Redcedar knows that Azara is wasting no time. He's just seen that her boggarts are more powerful than ever. He also knows that Golden Wood isn't yet ready for war.

"But the sea elves *are* ready to fight. They have to be. It's their job to protect the Fairy Realm from enemies on the borders. They are also the best elf warriors in the realm. And they have the best spies. Birds and other creatures all along the river and throughout the forest report to Lord Chiton. It won't take him long to find your grandmother. And when he does, we will move at once. I promise you, we will rescue Queen Rose."

"But Azara could kill my grandmother before we can save her..."

"We're doing our best to go to her aid as fast as we can." Captain Cottonwood said. "If it helps, I don't believe Azara will kill her right away. I suspect she intends to use her as a bargaining tool. You've got to trust me. It's already getting dark. It will take us all night to reach the sea elves. We've got to get going."

For a moment she continued to hesitate, and then she straightened up and looked him in the eye.

"All right," she said. "I'll follow you. But we've got to hurry."

CHAPTER EIGHT

Autumn flew above the narrow path that led to the sea as Captain Cottonwood ran below. The forest was dense here, very little light came from above, and the air hung heavy and still.

As she swerved to dodge trees and bushes, Autumn felt as if she was re-living her flight through the storm. Only this time she did *not* want to run into a boggart. So she did her best to peer into the darkness as she went whizzing by.

They'd traveled for a long while, without even pausing to catch their breath, when the elf warrior suggested they stop to rest beside a small stream. He didn't have to say it twice. Autumn no sooner heard his words, than she realized she was not only tired, she was starving. So she slowed her pace and fluttered to a nearby blackberry bush. There she pulled a spider web scarf from her pack and began to fill it with berries. Meanwhile Captain Cottonwood found a bluebell plant that was still blooming, picked a pair of the bell-shaped flowers, and filled them with water from the stream.

Autumn sighed as she settled beside him under the prickly vines of the blackberry bush. Her wings and shoulders ached so much she could barely move. She slumped forward to rest her head on her upraised knee. When she started to doze off, she immediately jerked herself wake.

"There's no time for you to sleep," the elf warrior told her. "We've got to get to the sea elves."

"You don't need to tell me that," she said, in her haughtiest princess voice. "I'm perfectly fine."

"Great," he replied, hiding a smile. "Have some water."

He handed her a bluebell cup of water, and she pushed the sack of berries in his direction.

They'd nearly finished their meal when Autumn abruptly broke the silence to ask a question that had been on her mind since she heard the news of Azara's escape.

"Your folk in the North Woods held Azara captive for a long time. You must know a lot about her. Tell me what she's like."

"I have no idea. I don't think anyone understands Azara, except perhaps your grandmother. Azara's her niece, after all."

Autumn looked away. "Gran doesn't talk about her."

After a moment she looked back at him. "Related or not, my grandmother hates Azara. Which isn't surprising since Azara killed her only child. The problem is…I was so young when it happened,

I don't remember anything…except for my mother… I have a faint memory of her…*a fragment of a lullaby…a gentle feeling as she held me…a sense of being loved*…But beyond that all I know is my parents were great warriors, that they led the rebellion against Azara, and that she killed them."

"I was just a boy at the time of the uprising myself," the elf warrior said after a moment. "My father was a commander in Lord Blackcedar's army. He was killed in battle by Azara's boggarts. My mother died when I was born, but I'd always felt close to her because my father talked about her all the time. When he died, it was like I lost them both. In a way, we were both orphaned by Azara."

Autumn abandoned her princess attitude.

"I'm sorry," she said.

"You don't need to feel sorry," the elf warrior told her. "Lord Blackcedar took me in and gave me a home. He was good to me. He always made sure I had everything I needed…but it wasn't like having a home, or a family, of my own…"

For a moment Autumn was quiet. When she spoke, her voice was so soft he had to lean forward to hear.

"You must have been lonely. I was lucky. I had Gran. But I still missed my parents." She looked down at her hands.

"Your parents were fighting to save the realm."

"Yes, I know," she swallowed. "Just like your father."

"I know they didn't intend to leave me," she went on after a moment. "They didn't know they would die. And it *was* their duty…

after all, my mother was a member of the royal family…and the fairy folk had begged my parents for help…but still…"

"You needed them."

She glanced up at his face and a look of understanding passed between them. Then she got to her feet and shook out her wings. "Well, Captain Cottonwood, I think it's time for us to get going if we're going to rescue my grandmother."

"Call me Lance," he said. "I think we know each other now."

CHAPTER NINE

A fresh wind carrying the salty tang of the sea greeted them when Autumn and Lance reached the coast the next morning. Rolling sand dunes dotted with clumps of waving grasses stretched out before them, and they heard the restless sound of the breaking waves. Now and then a grey and white gull soared overhead, intent on some purpose of its own.

All at once a dozen sea elves appeared from behind a nearby dune to block their way. Wearing uniforms of black and silver, they had stern faces and carried spears tipped with the teeth of barracudas. Pushing back her wings and straightening her shoulders, Autumn landed on the path and stepped forward to confront the formidable warriors. She hoped they were friendlier than they appeared. She didn't much care for the look of their spears.

The sea elves snapped to attention and bowed stiffly to Autumn.

"Welcome to the land of the sea elves, your Highness," the group's leader said. "I am Captain Willet Bayberry. The birds brought us word that you were coming. We are here to lead you and Captain Cottonwood to Lord Chiton."

"Thank you, Captain Bayberry," Autumn replied.

The sea elves turned and began to march across the dunes toward the breakers. Lance strode along beside the sea elf captain while Autumn flew just above. Sand blew against the elves as they moved, but the headwind presented an even greater problem for Autumn. Already tired from their nightlong journey through the forest, she had to beat her wings with more force than ever to battle the powerful onshore breeze.

"We're nearly to the beach," Captain Bayberry called up to her. "Once we're on the hard sand we can move faster. Would you like us to slow down a little now?"

"Certainly not," she responded, determined not to show any weakness in front of these fierce warriors, though the effort needed to fly against the wind hurt her already aching back and shoulders. Still she could fly faster than she could run.

To Autumn the minutes seemed like hours. At last they crossed the final row of dunes and saw a broad, flat beach stretched out before them. The sun shone on the water, which sparkled in response. Nothing but the rise and fall of the waves interrupted the endless blue expanse between the shore and the horizon. In all her travels, Autumn had never before seen the sea.

The elves followed a footpath to the beach. There they turned northward and began to run across the flat sand beside the water. Autumn was captivated by her first glimpse of the breakers. She climbed higher and higher so she could gaze at the deep blue waves crashing on the sand, see the white salt spray burst high in the air, and hear the booming echo as the ocean surged onto the shore. The sea's beauty and power overwhelmed her.

"Are you coming?" a voice called from below. Lance had stopped to wait for her.

"Yes, of course," Autumn responded, startled out of her trance. She looked down and realized that in her distraction she had fallen behind. She fluttered down to elf level. "I had no idea it would be like this. I've never seen anything so amazing. Does it ever end?"

Captain Bayberry had halted his troop and waited for them to join him.

"We've sent ships out to look for the other side," he said, over-hearing her question. "But no one has ever found it, although occasionally an albatross reports reaching another shore."

"It's amazing. Someday when all this is over, I'll come back," Autumn said as they resumed their trek.

It wasn't long before they arrived at a towering castle. Shaped like a gigantic whelk shell, it twisted far above them, nearly reaching the top of the cliff that loomed beside the beach. The castle had a deep, cave-like opening for an entrance and walls that spiraled upward. At the top a beacon sent a beam of light far out to sea.

Autumn landed so she could walk with the others. As they approached, they saw sea elves and sea maidens passing in and out of the castle in a steady stream. The maidens wore tunics as airy as beach foam draped over sea green body suits, outfits fashioned to allow them to swim swiftly through river or ocean. The elves wore similar suits, though theirs were black and topped by silver jackets that shone like fish scales. All walked swiftly and purposefully, many headed toward a long dock that stretched far out into the sea with a long line of ships tied alongside it. Some glanced curiously at the newcomers, but no one spoke to them.

Captain Bayberry led Autumn and Lance through the entrance. Inside a smooth white corridor wound around and around as it sloped gently upward. Their footsteps echoed as they ascended a long path. It ended at the very top before a large golden door. The captain knocked with the hilt of his sword.

"This is the headquarters of the Sea Elf Armada," Captain Bayberry said, turning to Autumn and Lance. "Lord Chiton is expecting you."

A uniformed sea elf opened the door and then stepped back to allow them to pass.

They entered a cavernous room that looked like the inside of an abalone shell, bare of any ornament, with shining silver walls and a vaulted ceiling. A large clam shell chair sat on a platform in the center. Small groups of two or three sea folk moved about the room, intent on their own purposes.

The sea elf seated on the chair wore a midnight blue robe with a chain of silver shells like stars around his neck. He had the lined face and piercing eyes of one who has spent a lifetime confronting the sun and wind. Long white hair bore witness to his years, but there was nothing frail about the elf lord that rose to face them.

"Welcome to the Land of the Sea Elves, Your Highness, Captain Cottonwood," Lord Chiton said in a deep voice. He bowed to Autumn, and nodded at Lance, before signaling for a pair of sea elves to bring two chairs. "I assume you are here because of Azara," he said once they were seated.

"That's right, I gather you heard from your spies," Autumn replied. "Yesterday Captain Cottonwood brought us the news of Azara's escape. Queen Rose immediately called for a council of war to be held at The Gathering Place. We were coming to tell you about it and to ask for your help in the battle against Azara, but now things have changed. Yesterday afternoon Azara's boggarts kidnapped my grandmother."

"The birds told us a boat was attacked on the river."

"Queen Rose was on that boat."

"I see," Lord Chiton said. His eyes narrowed. "It appears Azara has seized the advantage."

"For now perhaps," Lance put in. "But we are on our way to rescue Queen Rose. That's why we've come to you. We need your help."

"Of course," Lord Chiton replied. He turned to where Captain Bayberry stood nearby. "Inform Captain Marina of the situation. You'll find her onboard the *Wavedancer* in the harbor. Ask her to prepare her ship and two others for battle. Tell her I will send for her as soon as we are ready to formulate a plan."

The captain saluted and, with a parting nod to Lance and Autumn, left with his soldiers.

"It's been a long time since we've had a visitor from Golden Wood," Lord Chiton said, looking at Autumn. "I believe the last was your grandmother. She came not long after the death of your parents."

"My grandmother sent me here," Autumn said. "But I'm not sure why. Something about a golden tree. She said you would explain." She looked up at Lord Chiton with a question in her eyes, but when he didn't respond, she continued. "After she was kidnapped, I wanted to go at once to my grandmother's rescue. But Lord Redcedar said we needed to come here first."

"He was right. Your visit here is crucial if you wish to defeat Azara. But before I explain about the golden tree, let me tell you how we will help you rescue Queen Rose.

"To begin with, we will mobilize all the tribes, from the mightiest eagle to the tiniest field mouse. Our spy network is considerable.

Someone will discover where Azara is keeping your grandmother. As soon as we know where she is, I'll send three ships filled with sea elf warriors to help you free her.

"But the golden tree is the other matter we must discuss. Your grandmother sent you here because we sea elves guard the source of your family's power. Because of Azara's return, the time for you to claim your inheritance has arrived sooner than expected. What did your grandmother tell you of the golden tree?"

"Just that it exists somewhere deep within your land and that it can give me the strength I will need to confront Azara."

Lord Chiton nodded. "The tree holds a power that can help you both to defeat Azara and to rule the realm when you become queen. You will find it deep in a hidden grotto in a mountain here beside the sea. It is guarded by a wood sprite named Forsythia. She will teach you to use the tree's power."

Autumn didn't respond for a moment. Standing in this magnificent room, deep in the Land of the Sea Elves, she suddenly felt overwhelmed. Just because her mother was a warrior...and her grandmother...that didn't mean she knew how to fight.

She looked at Lord Chiton. His solemn face made it clear. She had no choice. As the future queen of the Realm the fight against Azara was *her* fight.

"Gran taught me that the queen of the Fairy Realm should rule with compassion and justice, not violence," she said. She paused and then added in a determined voice, "Nevertheless, if it is my duty to lead this fight, then lead it I will."

Autumn glanced at Lance. He nodded and sketched a salute. She looked back at the lord of the sea elves.

"How do I find the grotto?"

CHAPTER TEN

The next morning Lance found Autumn already waiting beside the castle entrance. Her arms were crossed and her body was tense as she gazed toward the ocean.

"Are you ready?"

She turned to look at him.

"I am," she said. "But I have to admit I'm nervous. One moment I'm healing trees in the forest, and the next I'm on my way to rescue my grandmother from Azara and her boggarts. I always knew I'd be queen someday. But I didn't expect it to come so soon. I'm not afraid of danger. I can deal with that. But I am afraid of failing. Fairy folk will die if I don't defeat Azara. And my grandmother will be first."

"All I know is you had what it took to overcome the storm, to stand up to a boggart, and to be willing to follow your grandmother up river," Lance said. "You have plenty of courage. You just need to learn the skills of a warrior. I'll help you with that. And so will the sea elves. But first you've got to find that tree."

"Then I guess we'd better follow the dragonfly," Autumn said, indicating a large blue and green dragonfly that hovered just in front of the castle. "She appears to be our guide."

The rapid beat of the dragonfly's wings sent humming waves of sound in all directions. They washed over Autumn and Lance as they approached. When she saw them drawing near, the regal creature drew herself up to a vertical position, and greeted them in a beautiful melodious voice.

"Good morning, your Highness," she said. "And good morning Captain Cottonwood. Lord Chiton has asked me to guide you both to the grotto in the cliff. If you are ready, we can go now."

Autumn nodded and the dragonfly turned and started out across the golden sandy beach. Autumn and Lance followed close behind. Although it was smooth going at first, it wasn't long before the trail began to rise. Large boulders lined the path. Occasionally they passed huge cypress trees, bent and twisted by the wind. After a while the path wound around to the other side of the hill. The terrain became browner and more barren, the air much warmer without the breeze from the sea.

When they had traveled for quite some time, the dragonfly paused and settled onto an out cropping of rock beside the path. A dignified nod of her head indicated they were to sit on a pair of rocks beside her.

"How are you doing?" the large insect asked in her unique and lovely voice. Now that they were seated close to the dragonfly, they could see the beauty of her intense colors. Her chest was green, her abdomen purple, and her long transparent wings were slightly tinged with yellow at the ends.

"A trifle warm, perhaps, but otherwise all right," Autumn answered.

"I've been moving slowly so you could follow. Normally I would have reached the top of the cliff long ago."

"Is it much farther?" Lance asked.

"We'll soon reach the mouth of the cave," the dragonfly replied. "I thought this would be a good place to stop."

She leaned toward them and lowered her voice. "I thought you should know that you're being followed."

Startled Autumn and Lance looked behind them.

"Ever since we set out, something has crept along behind us. It stays close to the ground, and looks like a rock, but it's a rock that moves with us."

"It must be a boggart," Lance said.

"That's what I suspect," the dragonfly responded. "I already put out the word that we might need assistance. If you want it, help is in place. I just have to give the signal.

"Oh yes," Autumn said. "Please do!"

The dragonfly zipped high in the air, spun around twice, then resumed leading them up the path. Autumn and Lance followed. A short time later, they stopped again. Suddenly angry shrieks filled the air. Autumn and Lance spun around.

From a ledge above the path behind them, several large spiders had dropped long, sticky threads which other spiders on the ground were furiously wrapping around a sandstone-colored creature. A huge tarantula stood beside them, waiting to inject its poison into the captive boggart.

"Wait!" Lance shouted.

"Let me question it first," he said, turning to Autumn. "I've interrogated many a prisoner since I've been in Lord Blackcedar's army. Perhaps I can get it to tell me where Azara is holding Queen Rose."

Lance ran to the place where the spiders waited with their captive with Autumn close behind. They both looked down at the angry creature tied at their feet. The boggart glared back at them.

Autumn was surprised to see that this boggart didn't look nearly as dangerous as the one that attacked her in the forest. This boggart had pale blue eyes, colorless eyebrows, a pointed nose above a narrow mouth, grey skin, and wispy hair. It wore a tunic made from a soft, indistinct material that seemed to be no color or all colors.

"When that tarantula sinks her teeth into you, you'll die," Lance told the boggart,

He leaned over him and pulled out his sword. "Your only hope is to tell us where Azara is holding Queen Rose."

The boggart spat on the ground. "I have nothing to say."

"If that's the way you want I," Lance said agreeably. I'd just as soon rid the realm of another boggart. I doubt if you're of much consequence anyway. In fact you probably don't know anything at all."

"I know plenty. For instance I know that when we kidnapped Queen Rose, you and your friends were powerless to protect her."

"Everyone in the realm knows about that," Lance scoffed, ignoring the boggart's comment about the elves being helpless. "If you were really of any value to Azara, you'd know where they are."

"I do know," the boggart sneered.

"Then tell us!" Lance held his sword to the boggart's throat.

The boggart didn't respond. The tarantula moved in and stood over the captive. It's long, dagger-like fangs raked the boggart's body.

"Get that thing away from me!"

Autumn leaned forward.

"Where is Azara holding Queen Rose?"

The boggart refused to answer.

The tarantula's long tongue began to lick the boggart's face. "Mmm, this will make a tasty meal," the giant spider said and settled down beside the boggart.

The other spiders cheered the tarantula on.

"Kill it! Kill it!" they cried.

The tarantula clasped the boggart's neck with its fangs and began to squeeze.

"Stop! Stop! I'll tell you."

The tarantula paused, but when the boggart didn't speak, he squeezed its neck again.

"Head up river!" the boggart gasped. "They're in a cave below the river bank."

The tarantula eased its hold.

"Where on the river?" Lance demanded.

But the boggart closed his eyes and acted as if he'd passed out.

Angrily Lance pushed the tarantula aside and reached out to grasp the boggart by the throat. But just as he clutched at the creature's clammy skin, the boggart morphed into a long, slender snake. Before Lance could stop him, he slid out of the spiders' bonds and disappeared into a crevice in the cliff. His voice echoed back to them.

"You fools. You'll never defeat Azara."

"That went well," Autumn said, her hands on her hips as she glared at Lance and the tarantula. "Remind me to always put you two in charge of interrogations."

"He isn't going anywhere," Lance replied. "As soon as he leaves that crevice, he'll be a tasty meal for a falcon named Peregrine. It's been watching over us ever since we left the castle of the sea elves. As for finding Queen Rose, I'll admit I would have liked to get more information out of him, but all is not lost. I have faith in Lord Chiton's network of spies. They'll soon discover where Rose is being held, without the help of any boggart."

Autumn sniffed and went to rejoin the dragonfly. Lance followed and the three of them resumed their ascent. They soon came to a sharp turn that cut deep into the side of the cliff. A shadow hung over this section of the path, and it was hard to see beyond a huge rock that sat squarely in the center.

"Here we are," the dragonfly said. "The entrance is behind that rock."

"It's awfully dark," Autumn observed as she cautiously approached the opening.

"Don't worry," a squeaky voice piped up from the entrance almost at their feet. "The fireflies will light the way."

Startled, Autumn and Lance looked down. In the shadow of the cave's entrance they could just make out the form of a tiny ground beetle.

"Ah, there you are," said the dragonfly. "Is everyone in place?"

"Oh yes," the beetle replied. "My relatives are scattered throughout the tunnel. They will shout out a warning if anyone tries to follow Princess Autumn and Captain Cottonwood. And the fireflies are waiting to guide them."

"That should do it," Autumn said. Then she turned to the dragonfly.

"You've helped us so much, and we don't even know your name."

"Dahlia," the dragonfly replied in her melodious voice.

"Thank you, Dahlia," Autumn said.

The dragonfly gave a gracious nod of her head before Autumn turned to enter the cave.

"I can't see a thing," Lance said as they stepped through the entrance.

"Take another step," the little voice piped up.

Autumn and Lance moved into the darkness. All at once flashing lights lit up the tunnel. They could see the way ahead was straight and level.

Autumn and Lance hurried to keep up with the fireflies. All went well until the tunnel abruptly ended at the smoothest wall Autumn had ever seen. There wasn't a crack or rough spot anywhere.

"Oh my!" Autumn said. "How ever does it open?"

"That's what we've been wondering," said a tiny beetle at her feet. "We checked all along the bottom of the wall, but we couldn't find any sign of a door."

Lance beat on the wall several times with his fist, but there wasn't any response. So he kicked the bottom. But all he got from that was a sore toe. Next he began to walk the length of the wall, pausing periodically to knock on it, first up high, then in the middle, then down low. Finally he got down on his knees and peered along the bottom, looking for some sign of a crack. Frustrated he turned to Autumn.

"There must be a secret way to open the door," he said.

While Lance had been trying to find a way to break through the wall, Autumn had simply stood still and gazed at it.

"Maybe it's a spell," she suggested. "This is a magic place, after all. Perhaps there's something we're supposed to say."

"Like what?"

"I don't know." I can't believe Gran sent me here without telling me how to get in…wait a minute…maybe…

Autumn started to sing.

"*Magic doorway to my dream,*

Cool me with yon fragrant stream,

Shelter me with leaves of gold,

Guide me till my story's told."

The rock slid back. They walked through and found themselves standing at the entrance to a golden grotto.

"How did you do that?"

"It's a lullaby my grandmother used to sing to me. She always said it would open the door to my dreams."

Lance motioned her forward. "Here's your secret grotto."

He watched from the entrance as she stepped into the light.

CHAPTER ELEVEN

Golden light filled the grotto. The sun shone from above, slipping through a natural skylight high on the mountain. The walls, smooth and white as polished marble, glowed with an iridescence of their own. A clear stream added the gentle sound of running water, and the floor was covered by lush green grass.

A golden tree stood in the center. It had the softly bending branches of a willow, but its slender leaves were a lustrous gold. They shimmered in the light like golden coins. It was small, more like a gentle apple tree than a mighty oak. Its branches swayed as if blown by a breeze, yet the air in the grotto was completely still.

As Autumn stepped into the sunlight, the tree stopped moving. Autumn stood still as well. The feeling in the grotto was powerful and gentle at the same time. It came from the tree. Autumn had tended trees all her life, but she'd never encountered one like this.

She reached out to touch the tree and it leaned forward in response, enfolding the tiny fairy in its golden branches. The experience brought back a memory she hadn't even known she possessed. Being held by the tree felt just like being held in her mother's arms. She closed her eyes and let herself be drawn into its golden warmth.

Just then someone emerged from behind the tree. It was Forsythia, the tree sprite her grandmother had mentioned. She had long fair hair, deep violet eyes, and wore a pale green gown. Her face was solemn, but her eyes were kind. She spoke with a voice as golden as the tree.

"Welcome, my child," she said.

Autumn stood up straight.

"Hello, Forsythia."

"The birds told me you were coming. I understand you have need of my magic."

"Lord Chiton said you could help me in my fight against Azara."

"Indeed I can, but first tell me why you seek to confront her."

An anxious look immediately replaced the peaceful expression on Autumn's face. "She's kidnapped my grandmother and I've got to rescue her."

"I would have thought the army of Lord Blackcedar or the Armada of the sea elves could do that more effectively than a mere slip of a girl, even if she is the future queen of the Fairy Realm." She watched to see Autumn's reaction to her words.

Autumn stepped away from the tree. "The sea elves have promised to help, but it's my responsibility to rescue my grandmother. What sort of queen will I be if I let others fight my battles?"

"I see you're as brave as I have been told," Forsythia replied. "But there is something you need to know. Azara's power is as great as it is because she also possesses a branch of this golden tree."

Forsythia sat down on the grass and motioned for Autumn to join her.

"This isn't an ordinary tree. It's magic has served your family for generations. All the rulers of the realm have used its power, including Azara.

"Many years ago she came to me for help just as you are doing. She wanted a branch to increase her power. She promised to use it for the good of the realm. But instead she used it for evil. She forced her subjects to work in her mines and treated them like slaves. The folk of the realm lived in dreadful poverty, while Azara accumulated great wealth. Because of the power she gained from the branch, no one could stop her. Your parents tried, but they didn't have a chance. In fact, she used the branch to destroy them."

As she spoke, the tree became agitated, its branches jerking from side to side. Forsythia gently reached to stroke the trunk in an effort to calm it. Then she turned her attention back to Autumn.

"It's time for you to learn the truth about Azara and your parents," Forsythia said. "If you are going to fight her, you must understand how cruel she is. I know this will be hard, but I must tell you how your parents died. A pair of sparrows told me. They saw it all.

"Your parents were on their way to ask for Lord Chiton's help in the rebellion against Azara. Their mission was supposed to be secret, but they were betrayed.

"The marshes on the border between Golden Wood and the Land of the Sea Elves were toxic, poisoned by waste from Azara's mines. As your parents flew above them, Azara used her branch to make the mud boil. Poisonous fumes rose from its depths. They formed a black cloud so huge it shut out the light of the sun."

As Forsythia spoke the light in the grotto dimmed.

"A group of boggarts suddenly sprang up in front of your parents. They flung a gigantic net over both Hawk and Marigold. Your parents were trapped. They flew back and forth, looking for a way to escape, but the net held firm."

Autumn clenched her hands in her lap. She wanted Forsythia to stop, but she knew she had to hear what the tree sprite would say.

"When the sparrows saw what was happening they tried to raise a corner of the net to let your parents out, but a boggart spotted them. He hit them with an arm as hard as a tree trunk and sent them spinning. They landed on the ground not far away. Marigold saw what happened to the birds. She flew as near to them as she could, and begged them to deliver a final message.

'Tell Autumn we love her,' she said. 'Ask my mother to keep her safe!'"

As the wood sprite spoke, tears gathered in Autumn's eyes and slipped silently down her face.

"Then Marigold flew back to Hawk. As your parents were forced closer and closer to the mud, they cried out for help. But no one came. When they saw the end was near, Hawk put his arms around your mother and held her tight. They died the moment they hit the poisoned ground."

In the sudden silence, Autumn could barely breathe. Overcome by grief, she covered her face with her hands and wept.

Forsythia's eyes filled with pity as she took Autumn's hands in her own. The tree reached out with its long, slender branches and wrapped Autumn and Forsythia in golden leaves. Slowly light returned to the grotto.

"I'm sorry," Forsythia said at last. "But you had to know. You've got to understand how wicked she is. There is no mercy in Azara. She is ruthless.

"You also need to know about the power I am about to give you. This magic can be used for evil as well as good. Azara used it for great evil indeed."

She paused to make sure Autumn was ready for her to go on.

"After your parents died, your grandmother came to me. Rose knew the story of the golden tree. She believed it was the source of Azara's power. She realized she would need a branch of her own if she was to defeat her wicked niece. So I gave her one, and she used it to drive Azara from the fairy realm." Here the tree rustled gently.

"But Rose had learned a lesson from Azara. She didn't want to risk being overwhelmed by her own dark side. So when Azara had been defeated, your grandmother brought back her branch.

"Unfortunately she didn't do the same with Azara's. She took it away, but instead of destroying the branch, she gave it to Lord Blackcedar. He locked it away on Ice Mountain. Recently a traitor stole it and returned it to Azara. That was how she escaped. And that is how she intends to recapture the throne.

"Now we come to you. If I give you a branch, what will you do? If you confront Azara and live, will you keep the branch? And if you do, how will you use it?"

Autumn was shocked. How could Forsythia think she could be like Azara?

But Forsythia just looked at her. In the face of her scrutiny Autumn was silent. Though she remained outwardly calm, she was filled with confusion. She didn't believe she'd ever do anything evil. She was a healer. She always had been. And yet she and Azara were part of the same family. Did she really know what she might be capable of? She thought it over for a moment then she looked Forsythia straight in the eye.

"I don't believe I could ever be like Azara," she told Forsythia. "But I can't predict what the future will bring. Everyone has a dark side. Of course I can't know for sure. But I don't believe I would ever be ruled by mine."

Forsythia looked deep into Autumn's eyes. "I don't see anything of Azara's greed in you," she said. "But I do see your grandmother's compassion."

Forsythia reached out to the tree, which leaned toward her. She gently broke off a small branch and handed it to Autumn.

"A powerful force flows through the branches of this tree," Forsythia said. "But it can only be used by a member of the royal family. Autumn, this branch belongs to you. When the time comes, you will find the way to send out its fire. It requires a strong will to control it. Now go. You have what you came for. Use it well."

Autumn reached out and took the branch.

Though it had been broken off, the branch still felt as if it were part of the living tree. There was a faint glow to the wood, like the gentle light in the evening sky. Autumn held the branch tenderly, filled with wonder at its beauty.

"And is this elf going with you?" Forsythia asked. She indicated Lance waiting in the doorway.

"Yes, Forsythia," Autumn answered. She gestured for Lance to come forward. "This is Captain Lanceleaf Cottonwood."

"Tell me," Forsythia asked as Lance stood before her. "How did you become involved in this?"

"I'm an emissary for Lord Blackcedar," Lance answered. "He sent me to warn the folk in the Fairy Realm of Azara's escape. Autumn and I were on our way to the Land of the Sea Elves when her grandmother was kidnapped. Now I believe it's my duty to help her rescue Queen Rose." He looked at Autumn. "Actually it's more than my duty; it's what I want to do."

"That's very brave of you," the wood sprite said. "You must realize by now how dangerous her fight is going to be."

"I have my own reason for wanting Azara defeated," Lance told her. "She was responsible for the death of my father."

"Then you have my blessing," Forsythia said. "Autumn will need the assistance of a brave companion. Now you must both be on your way. No time can be lost if you are to save Rose."

When Autumn and Lance reentered the tunnel both were aware that somewhere in the realm Azara was waiting.

CHAPTER TWELVE

As soon as they returned to the castle, Autumn and Lance met with Lord Chiton.

"Your return is well-timed," he told them. "My spies believe they have found the place where your grandmother is being held. It's time to meet with Captain Marina and Captain Bayberry. We must devise a plan."

While Lance went to fetch the two sea elves, Autumn decided to walk along the ocean. The beach struck her as a good place to sort out the unexpected events of the past two days.

Mesmerized by the waves and the sun sparkling on the water, she let herself drift in the warmth of the moment.

Reality hit like a crashing boulder when a voice whispered in her ear.

"Silly girl, did you really think we wouldn't find you?"

Autumn whirled around. A dragonfly was hovering just behind her, but it wasn't Dahlia. Its voice was cold, its body dark, its eyes cruel, and the sound of its wings whirred with menace. She knew at once it was a boggart. Too late Autumn recognized the danger of coming here alone. She tried to call for help, but there was no one in sight.

"Azara has sent her spies to search for you. Now that I have found you, I intend to kill you."

Autumn looked the boggart full in the face. Locking onto his eyes, she drew on every particle of strength she had.

"I'm not afraid of you," she announced, her voice as strong as she could make it. "Get out of my way."

"I don't think so," the boggart said. "You're in my power now."

"That's what you think."

Autumn raised her arm and pointed the branch directly at the boggart. Suddenly the shape-shifting creature wasn't a dragonfly anymore. Now a rat scuttled away across the sand. Autumn aimed her branch and willed a flame of energy to strike the boggart. The blast fell short, and the boggart ran faster. She aimed again. The boggart vanished in a puff of smoke.

"So that's how it works," she said aloud. "I'd better be more careful. I can't just kill things."

"Why not? They'd kill you."

Autumn spun around and discovered she was being addressed by a very plump, very prickly hedgehog. He was obviously a youngster because he was small, not even half the size he would be when he was fully grown.

"Get back! Didn't you see what I just did? Do you want me to kill you too?"

"No, stop! I'm no boggart. I'm a messenger."

But Autumn was still suspicious. The last boggart had surprised her. She didn't intend to be caught again.

"How do I know that? If you're not a boggart, who are you? And what are you doing here? This is no place for a hedgehog."

"I've been looking for you," he answered. "And you haven't been easy to find. It took me all night to get here. I've had a heck of a time walking across this beach. I've got sand all over me." He tried to shake himself off, but only succeeded in picking up more.

Autumn frowned. "So what is this message you have for me?"

"It's about your grandmother."

"What! Where is she? Is she all right?"

"She's all right, or at least she was. But she's in great danger. She needs to be rescued right away."

"Come with me, we must tell Lord Chiton," Autumn said, and set off toward the castle.

"Wait a minute," the hedgehog cried out. "I can't fly, you know."

"Sorry." She returned to the side of the prickly fellow and began to shepherd him along as patiently as she could. Despite her attempt to go slow, he was puffing and panting.

"I've never done anything like this before," he told Autumn between gasps. "I was told to get here as fast as I could. And I did. But dashing about really isn't for me. We hedgehogs like to take our time. The world has so much to sniff and munch on."

Autumn paused. For the first time she looked carefully at the new arrival. She could see his quills were all in disarray, and his little black nose was sticking out from a face covered with sand. He kept trying to wipe it with his paws, but they were sandy too and he only got in more of a mess.

She smiled. "Let me help," she said. Hovering beside him, she gently wiped his face with a handkerchief she took from her pocket. "There, how's that?"

"Much better," he replied, looking happier. "Thank you very much."

"Are you ready now" she asked.

"Oh yes," he replied.

"This way then," Autumn said. When they arrived at the entrance to the sea elf castle, it was clear the hedgehog was too large to fit inside. So Autumn told him to wait while she went to get Lord Chiton. She flew up the corridor as fast as she could and knocked on the door. It was opened by a sentry and Autumn rushed in.

"Lord Chiton," she cried. "There's a hedgehog at the castle entrance with a message from my grandmother!"

Lord Chiton had been talking to Lance, Captain Bayberry, and another tall sea elf. Now he turned to Autumn.

"A message about Rose? We must hear it at once."

The lord of the sea elves stood up and strode down the corridor, followed closely by the others. They found the hedgehog immediately outside.

"What's this I hear?" the lord of the sea elves said to him. "You have a message from Queen Rose?"

"Yes, your Lordship," the hedgehog replied.

"Then speak up, Mr. Hedgehog, but first, tell us your name."

"My name is Thorn," the hedgehog replied.

"Now then, Thorn, how was Rose when you left her?'

"Well, I didn't exactly leave her," the hedgehog replied. "This is more of a word of mouth message. You see, I heard it from a mockingbird who heard it from a mole who heard it from a gopher. It was the gopher who found Rose."

"Yes, yes, fine, but where did he find her?" the Lord Chiton asked, with more than a little impatience.

"She's being held in a cave in the riverbank. The entrance is concealed behind a pile of rocks near the water. The gopher that found her dug his way in from above."

"But where is this cave?" Autumn asked. "Does the message say how to find it?"

"Of course," the hedgehog replied. "That's why I'm here. I can take you to the very place."

"Wait a minute," Lance interjected. "How do we know this message is real? It could be a trap. The gopher could have been a boggart. And I have another question, just how did this hedgehog know where to find Autumn? She's from Golden Wood, not the Land of the Sea Elves? How did he know to come here?"

"That's a good question. Tell us Thorn, how did you know Princess Autumn would be here?" Lord Chiton asked.

"Her grandmother told the gopher Autumn was on her way to the Land of the Sea Elves," Thorn responded. "When I saw a fairy come out of the castle and fly across the sand, I knew it had to be Autumn. Sea elves don't fly." The hedgehog looked quite proud of this piece of logical deduction.

"That sounds reasonable," Lance said. "His message fits with the other information we have. The boggart we spoke to on the trail told us to follow the river, and the message from your spies reported she was in a cave on the river bank."

"I agree," the lord of the sea elves said. "Still, I'm glad to see you are being so careful. Boggarts can morph into anything."

"I wish we had a way to identify them," Autumn said.

"Your branch will tell you. When you aim the branch at a boggart, it vibrates."

Autumn looked thoughtful. She had noticed when she first met the dragonfly boggart on the beach that the branch was shaking. She'd thought it was just because she was nervous. But maybe it was because the branch was vibrating a warning. Before she could tell Lord Chiton what had happened, he brought forward the other sea elf that had been standing quietly at Captain Bayberry's side.

"Autumn and Thorn, I want you both to meet the commander of the ships who will help you to rescue Queen Rose."

Autumn looked up at the commander who towered over her just as the other sea elves did, and who looked every bit as fierce. Only this was not a sea elf, but a sea maiden.

"I am Captain Marina," the newcomer announced.

"How do you do," Autumn replied. Puzzled, she gazed into the sea maiden's face. Captain Marina looked familiar, but Autumn couldn't think why. Then she glanced at the lord of the sea elves. Of course, Captain Marina looked just like Lord Chiton. She had the same piercing eyes and the same nose.

Captain Marina smiled.

"Yes," she said, in response to Autumn's unspoken question. "I am Lord Chiton's daughter."

"A pair of crows just reported they observed increased boggart activity near the Great Falls," Lord Chiton told the hedgehog. "Is that near the place you have come to tell us about?"

"Yes indeed," Thorn answered.

"If you know where she is, we must go at once," Autumn said.

"Hold on a minute. We can't go until we have a plan," Lance pointed out.

"Our hedgehog friend is too large to travel on an elf ship," Lord Chiton said. "So Thorn, Princess Autumn, Captain Cottonwood and Captain Bayberry will have to travel by land. As the senior military officer in the group, I suggest Captain Cottonwood be in charge of planning the rescue itself, with your approval, of course," he said with a nod at Autumn.

"I think that's an excellent idea," Autumn agreed. "Captain Cottonwood knows far more about military strategy than I do."

"As for the sea elves, Captain Marina has prepared three ships for battle. It will be her task to attack from the river, kill as many boggarts as possible, and provide a distraction while the rescue party enters the cave.

"Now those of you traveling by land had best leave immediately. You must be in place before the ships arrive and they will arrive the day after tomorrow. We can't delay any longer. Queen Rose is in grave danger. Azara has vowed to kill her, and that is one promise Azara will keep."

CHAPTER THIRTEEN

A short time later, Autumn, Lance, and Captain Bayberry met in front of the castle. Both elves were armed with swords, plus Lance had a bow and quiver of porcupine quill arrows which he wore slung across his back. Autumn grasped the magic branch. They were soon joined by Thorn, who was brushing walnut crumbs off his round little belly.

"Do we have far to go?" Autumn asked the hedgehog.

"Indeed we do," Thorn replied. "We'll have to travel all night."

"Then we'd better get started," Autumn said.

Dahlia joined them as they were about to set off.

"I'm going with you," she announced. "Once you're in position on the riverbank, I'll return here and tell Lord Chiton. He'll give Captain Marina and the rest of the Armada the order to head upriver."

"Then the rescue party is complete," Lance said. "Time for us to go."

"Do you think Azara and her boggarts are waiting for us?"Autumn asked, as they headed across the dunes toward the forest.

"I'm sure they are," Lance answered. "That's the whole reason why Azara kidnapped Queen Rose. She expects you to come to her rescue. She intends to capture you as well and then get rid of you both.

"The closer we get to the cave, the more dangerous it will be. That's why we are going to stay off the main path as much as possible. If we can avoid Azara's spies, we'll have a better chance of surprising the sentries at the cave."

"The forest is full of Lord Chiton's watchers," Dahlia put in. "They'll warn us if they spot any boggarts."

"That will help," Lance said. "But I still think we'd better travel cautiously. Boggarts can morph into just about anything. It makes them as good as invisible."

The rescue party soon reached the woods. Once they started to make their way through the trees, it became apparent they would have to do something about the little hedgehog. The undergrowth was thick, and there wasn't much light. Autumn, Dalhia and the elves could see clearly, but Thorn had difficulty perceiving anything beyond his nose. He exclaimed out loud as he bumped into one obstacle after another.

"I wonder if you could use the golden tree's branch to light Thorn's way," Lance whispered to Autumn. "If he could see better, he could go faster. As long as the light isn't too bright, I think it would be worth it. Just be sure you keep it low and focused on the ground."

"I'll give it a try," Autumn responded. Raising the branch she flew beside the hedgehog, giving him just enough light to see obstacles like tree roots and shrubs in his way.

"Thank you, Autumn," Thorn said in a relieved voice. "That helps a lot. I've bumped my poor nose way too many times already. And I really hate the prickles on those bushes. Just because my name is Thorn and I have quills all over my back, doesn't mean I like sharp objects sticking themselves in my face."

"Have you traveled this way before?" Autumn asked as they moved through the forest.

"Not until I came to find you," Thorn replied. "To be honest, I've never left the woods where I was born. Hedgehogs mostly just forage and eat. My life has never been very exciting. Not like this, not like going off to rescue the prisoner of an evil fairy queen! This is the most amazing thing anyone in my family has ever done."

Autumn was a little taken aback by his enthusiasm. She hoped he understood the danger involved in what they were doing.

"They're all very proud of me," the hedgehog went on. "I just hope I don't let them down." Suddenly he looked self-conscious as he focused his eyes on the ground. It was hard to tell through his fur, but Autumn thought he might be blushing.

"Actually," he continued, "There's one hedgehog in particular...her name is Peony... she's very pretty...she shared a strawberry with me once...at a hedgehog picnic...I'm sort of hoping she'll be impressed..."

"I don't think you need to worry about that," Autumn replied. "I'm sure she'll be very impressed indeed. And you've already accomplished your first goal. You found me didn't you? Now you just have to lead us to Azara's secret hiding place and your mission will be accomplished. But I think we'd best be quiet now. We don't want to alert any boggarts to our presence." Autumn smiled to herself. The little hedgehog seemed an unlikely hero but then why not?

After a while everyone's enthusiasm was dampened by their journey through the undergrowth. Not only did Thorn struggle to heave himself over one fallen log after another, but Autumn and Dahlia had to be alert to keep their wings from getting tangled in the webs of moss hanging from so many branches. Unable to make their way through huge clumps of impenetrable ferns, the entire party was forced to take endless detours, while prickly bushes and long, tangled vines appeared without warning, stabbing and tripping anyone who was careless or moved too fast. The journey continued hour after hour.

As the shadows lengthened into late afternoon, Autumn noticed Thorn was having a rough time. He staggered along bumping into rocks and tree trunks in spite of the light from the branch.

"I think Thorn needs a brief rest," she called out to Lance and Captain Bayberry, who were just ahead. "Let's stop for just a moment."

The two elf warriors came back to join them.

"That's a good idea," Lance said. "While Thorn rests, we'll scout around. We need to find out if the birds know anything more about the size of the force that is holding Queen Rose."

"I'll come with you," Dahlia said. "I can fly up high and see farther away."

"Be sure you stay out of sight," Captain Bayberry told Thorn.

"I will," Thorn murmured. He curled up under a holly bush and was asleep in seconds.

When Lance and Captain Bayberry had gone, Autumn looked about for a safe place to keep watch. She wanted to be where she could see Thorn, but she also wanted to be high enough to view the entire area. She spotted a large boulder covered in moss halfway up a nearby slope, and set out to establish a look out post there.

She flew to the top of the rock, and had just arranged the moss into a comfortable nest, when she felt the earth shake. The tremor dislodged the boulder and it began to roll forward, taking Autumn with it. She flung herself to the side but couldn't get far enough to be out of the way. The rock struck her and sent her careening backwards. She had barely begun to regain her balance when she was overtaken by a massive swarm of bees. Thrown into a panic when the earthquake shook their hive, the bees never even saw Autumn as they had swarmed over her. She dove toward a nearby hole in the ground in an attempt to escape and tumbled into darkness.

She screamed as she fell. It seemed like forever but she finally hit the bottom of the tunnel with a thud. Stunned, she tried to sit up and take in what had happened but she could hardly move. The tunnel was so narrow its walls closed in on her from every side. She looked around, but the light was too dim for even her powerful fairy eyes to see.

When Autumn looked upward she could just make out a distant and tiny circle of blue.

She struggled to stand up in the confined space. Once she was firmly on her feet, she put out her hands and turned around in a circle. She was trapped in a space so narrow she couldn't even open her wings. Hard walls of earth pressed in all around her.

"HELP!" she screamed. But no one answered. She tried again. Still no response.

She turned around again. The walls of earth pressed in all around her. There was no way out. She started to panic, but took a deep breath, and forced herself to be calm. That's when she remembered the branch. She'd put it on the ground while she arranged a place to sit. She hadn't picked it up when the earthquake hit so it was somewhere high above. She leaned against the wall and again took several deep breaths. She was trapped in a narrow tunnel far below the ground and she was starting to feel like she couldn't breathe.

She focused her mind on the branch. If only she hadn't dropped it.

All at once she had a vision of a frog pushing through the water, using its legs to swim. Of course, she would push against the walls the way a frog swims and make her way back up. She briefly wondered where the vision came from, if somehow it was sent by the branch, but she had no way to find out and besides, this was no time for questions. So she put her hands against the walls on either side, raised her right foot, and anchored it against the wall, then did the same with her left foot. Once both feet were firmly planted, she straightened her bent knees, and thrust herself upwards. She rose up a couple of inches. *YES!*

She held herself in place by pushing against the wall with her hands as she raised her feet again and again. It took all her strength, but after a few awkward attempts she got into a rhythm. She began to make her way upward, several inches at a time. She didn't stop to think about how far she had to go. She just pushed…and pushed.

It wasn't long before her arms and legs started to burn. Then she started feeling sick to her stomach. Her legs ached, her hands were bruised, and her back hurt…but she continued to work her way upward. She had to fight for every breath, and sweat dripped in her eyes, but she didn't take her hands off the wall. She had to get out of here. She had to rescue her grandmother.

As she became more aware of her surroundings, she realized she had probably fallen into an abandoned mole hole. The air in the tunnel had gotten fresher as she'd climbed, and she could tell she was almost at the top. The way out was almost in reach. She breathed a sigh of relief and with one last mighty push, hurled herself toward the edge of the opening. She grabbed for the rim, but she couldn't hold on. She slipped and fell back again into the darkness. *No!*

She flung out her hands out and pressed them against the wall. Rocks scraped her skin but she managed to slow her descent. She pressed harder…and harder…fighting for control. At last she stopped falling. For a moment she hung suspended, and then she took a deep breath. She raised her legs, pressed her feet against the wall, and began to climb once more. She refused to think about what had just happened. She didn't have time.

As she started to move upward tears of frustration slid down her face. If only she'd been more careful

It seemed as if she had been trying to make her way up that wall forever, when at last she reached the rim once more. This time she slowly reached out and carefully pulled herself up onto the ledge. It felt like she was moving in slow motion. Her wings hurt after being pressed so tightly against her body, but she managed to get them open. She sighed with relief when at last she half fluttered, half rolled onto solid ground.

Her entire body ached from the effort it had taken to climb back up. But there was no time to rest. She must find the branch and get back to Thorn. Lance and Captain Bayberry should have returned by now. They had to resume their journey. They had to rescue Gran.

She stood up and looked all around, but the branch was nowhere to be seen.

Where could it be?

In her mind's eye, she suddenly saw the branch lying against the trunk of a giant redwood tree. She opened her eyes and looked until she spotted a place that matched the picture in her mind. Sure enough, the branch was there.

She picked it up and flew as fast as she could back to Thorn.

The earthquake had woken him from his nap. He'd searched all over for Autumn, but couldn't find a sign of where she'd gone. Now he looked at his friend and his eyes as grew wide.

"Where have you been?" he asked in alarm.

"I fell down a mole hole," she told him. She looked down and for the first time noticed she was covered in dirt.

Just then Lance, Captain Bayberry and Dahlia came into view.

"Are you two all right?" Lance called out as they approached Autumn and Thorn. "Did you feel the earthquake?"

Then his eyes fell on Autumn and he stopped abruptly. "What happened to you?"

Thorn spoke up before she could answer.

"She fell down a mole hole," he told the others.

"Are you hurt?" Captain Bayberry asked.

"No, just a few scrapes and some dirt."

"You look awful," Lance said.

"I think you could have phrased that a little better," Dahlia told him, with a disapproving look.

Lance looked embarrassed. "That came out wrong," he said. "I didn't mean…tell us how you fell down a mole hole."

Autumn told them about the rock and the bees and her climb out of the hole. "Anyway, I got out of it," she concluded calmly.

"Good for you," Lance told her. "It can't have been easy."

"No, but enough about that," she replied. "We've got to be on our way."

With that, the rescue party resumed their trek to Azara's cave.

It was nearly dawn when they reached the riverbank. In the waning moonlight, they could just make out towering cliffs rising on both sides of the river. The Great Falls fell far and fast between them.

"This is the place," Thorn whispered. "Now what do we do?"

"First, I'll scout out the area," Lance told him. "Where exactly is the entrance to the tunnel?"

"It's at the foot of that cliff on the other side of the river. You'll see a tall pile of rocks. The entrance is behind them."

"I'll come with you" Autumn told Lance. "Azara will have guards watching the area. I can use the branch to tell which inno-cent looking objects are boggarts in disguise."

Lance and Autumn set off to investigate, while Captain Bayberry, Dahlia and Thorn waited among the trees. As Lance moved closer to the river bank, Autumn pointed the branch in every direction. Suddenly it began to vibrate.

Autumn silently indicated a pile of rocks on the other side of the river. A single rock was balanced on top.

"That one's a boggart," she whispered. "And there are others on the bank."

"They're guarding the entrance all right," Lance said when they rejoined the others. "They have a sentry stationed on a pile of rocks right in front of the entrance to the cave where they are holding Queen Rose, and more on the ground on either side."

"If we go a little farther downstream we could cross where the shadow of the cliff falls across the river. It would make us harder to see," Captain Bayberry said.

"Good idea," Lance told him. "Once we're on the other side, we'll figure out the next step in our plan."

Lance turned to the hedgehog.

"It's time for us to leave you, Thorn," he said. "Your task is done. You'd best be well away before the battle begins. Thank you for bringing the message and being our guide."

"Yes," Autumn agreed, giving the prickly hedgehog a careful hug. "Thank you. You've been a great help."

But Thorn had a different idea.

"I've been thinking it over. I want to help more if I can. I know you don't need me to go with you, but why don't I stay here? When you're ready to attack, give me a signal, and I'll take care of that boggart sentry on the rocks. I have time to fashion myself a bow. My quills are small and hard to remove, but if you lend me a few of your porcupine arrows, I could help when the battle begins." The little hedgehog looked hopefully at Lance.

"That's a great idea," Lance said as he reached for the quiver of arrows slung across his back. "You're welcome to use some of these. But you must promise to stay undercover. As soon as you fire off an arrow, Azara's forces will begin searching for you. Kill the sentry and get out of here before the boggarts kill you."

With that he and the others began to quietly move downriver. As soon as they found a place in the shadow of the cliff, Captain Bayberry and Lance quickly gathered twigs and cedar bark to make a canoe the two of them could use to cross the swift moving river.

"We'll split up now," Lance told Autumn and Dahlia. "The two of you should be able to fly across undetected. We'll set off as soon as you reach the other side. Wait there and watch for us. We'll be in the greatest danger when we are on the river. If they spot us, and we don't make it, you'll have to handle the rescue on your own."

"Maybe we could arrange some sort of a distraction," Autumn suggested. "We'll fly upriver and see if we can spot any fish. If we do, I'll ask them to create a commotion while you cross."

Without waiting for an answer, she and Dahlia flew away. They hadn't gone far when they spotted half a dozen large trout in a pool at the river's edge.

"Good morning," Autumn said softly as she hovered above them.

"Mmm, breakfast," the first trout replied, eyeing her hungrily.

"Hush, you silly fish," another told him. "Don't you know that's Princess Autumn?"

"Pardon our brother," another trout said. His size and voice of authority proclaimed him to be leader of the group. "He doesn't see so well," he added, smacking the first fish with his tail.

Autumn got right to the point.

"I need your help. Azara is holding Queen Rose prisoner in a cave on the other side of the river. Two elf warriors need to cross the river to help us rescue her. Could you splash about and make enough commotion to distract the boggarts while the elves row across?"

"Of course," the fish all bubbled in reply.

"Where and when?" the largest fish asked.

"As soon as I'm out of sight, head to the middle of the river. Have a fight or something to create a lot of noise just opposite that pile of rocks on the other side." She started to leave, then paused and looked back over her shoulder. "This dragonfly is with me. Don't eat her either."

Autumn raced back to Lance.

"It's all arranged," she told him. "Dahlia and I will go now. You two wait for a school of fish to create a lot of noise in the middle of the river," Autumn said. "That should distract the boggart sentries and make it safer for you to cross."

CHAPTER FOURTEEN

"Now that we're all here, what do we do next?" Captain Bayberry asked once all four members of the rescue party had safely gathered behind a huge oak tree on the other side of the river.

"We figure out how to get into the cave," Lance said.

"It looks like the entire boggart army is here," Dahlia pointed out.

"How in the realm will we get through them all?" Autumn asked. "If only there was another way in."

"I wish we could talk to the gopher that found Queen Rose in the first place," Lance said. "But I have no idea where to look for him."

"How about looking behind you?" a voice asked from somewhere near their feet.

Surprised, the rescue party spun around. For the first time they noticed a hole in the ground with a furry head sticking out of it. The fur was golden brown, the eyes were dark, and the nose twitched with curiosity.

"How long have you been there?" Captain Bayberry asked.

"I've kept watch ever since I put out the call for help," the gopher said. "I've been mighty worried about Queen Rose, especially since Azara turned up."

"So Azara's here is she?" Lance said. "I'm sorry to hear that. It would be easier if we only had boggarts to deal with."

As the gopher climbed out of his hole and came to greet them, Autumn realized he must be twice as big as she was. He seemed a little shy now that they were all standing face-to-face.

"I'm Autumn Primrose," she told the gopher, reaching out to shake his paw. She then introduced the others. "We've come because a hedgehog named Thorn told us you found my grandmother."

"Indeed I did, and she's a very nice fairy, I must say. Not at all as uppity as I thought queen might be. She's brave as well. She's in a pretty desperate situation, but it doesn't get her down. We had a nice little chat the day I found her. There weren't many boggarts around then, not like now. Now there are boggarts everywhere.

"My name's Dusty, by the way. I sent the message. But I was expecting more of you to come to the rescue. I don't see how the just four of you can take on Azara and her whole boggart army."

"We're also expecting three battle-ships loaded with sea elves," Lance told him.

Dusty looked relieved. "That's good," he said.

"Now we need to make a plan to rescue Queen Rose. It would help if you could draw a diagram of the cave where she is being held," Lance told the gopher.

Dusty found a sharp twig lying on the ground, and holding it with his two front paws, began drawing in the dirt.

"She's in a cave deep in the river bank," he said when he finished his drawing. "The cave has two entrances. On one side there's a tunnel that runs from the edge of the woods into the cave," he explained, pointing with the stick. "On the other side there's a tunnel that comes out of the cave onto the bank just above the river. She's chained to the wall in the middle.

"I suggest you enter the cave the way I did. There aren't any guards near the prisoner. They're all posted at the two tunnel entrances. If you follow the tunnel I dug into the cave from the top of the river bank, you'll come out right beside the prisoner."

"That sounds good to me," Autumn said. She looked around at the other three. All nodded in agreement.

"When do you expect the ships? I'll remove the dirt I piled around the entrance as soon as they come into view. I don't think Azara will notice anything with the sea elf Armada coming around the bend. Besides, there are bushes all around the tunnel entrance."

"If you've decided on your plan, I'll go and alert the Sea Elves. The ship could be here just after dawn tomorrow," Dahlia said. "Would that work?"

"It's fine with me," Lance said. "Can you be ready by then, Dusty?"

"Indeed I can."

"I have another suggestion," Captain Bayberry put in. "Ask Captain Marina to send a landing party ashore right before she rounds the bend. I'll meet them and lead them into the cave through the tunnel that comes from the woods. That way we can block any attempt by Azara to escape in that direction."

"Good idea," Lance said. "Got that, Dahlia?"

"Yes, Captain Cottonwood. I've got it."

"Go then," Lance told the dragonfly. "Tell Lord Chiton we're ready. And on your way, give the same message to Thorn. Tell him to fire his arrows at the sentry we pointed out as soon as the *Wavedancer* comes around the bend. Be sure he understands he must leave immediately when he's done that."

Dahlia gave a little salute, rose into the air and as her wings began to hum, took off across the river.

When Dahlia had vanished from sight, Dusty stood looking at the remaining rescuers. He clearly had something more to say.

"Is there something you want to add?" Lance asked.

"Well, yes," Dusty said. "There is something I think you should know. There happens to be another enemy you should be aware of, besides Azara, I mean."

"Who would that be?" Captain Bayberry asked.

"It's a snake," Dusty said. The gopher looked frightened just talking about it. "In fact, he's a gigantic snake. He could swallow any of us whole and still be hungry. Plus he's fast and silent and strikes without warning. I've seen his victims disappear before they even knew what was happening."

"What makes you think he's a threat to us?" Lance asked.

"Well, you see, this is his hunting ground," Dusty answered. "Of course, he isn't always here. He moves all over, really, but I just thought I'd mention him. There's always the possibility he could show up."

"Thanks for the warning," Lance told him. "But since there isn't anything we can do about the snake, we'd best figure out how to deal with Azara and hope we don't find ourselves with two enemies to deal with at once."

Autumn was silent as Lance, Captain Bayberry, and Dusty continued to discuss the details of the rescue plans. There was a frown between her eyes as she stared fixedly at the ground. She only looked up when the others started to move about.

With their plans complete, the rescuers gathered a meal of pine nuts and blackberries, and then settled down to rest until morning.

The other members of the rescue party soon fell asleep. Only Autumn remained sitting upright, her body tense as she gazed toward the river. Lance noticed, and guessing the reason, went to sit beside her. Neither said a word until Autumn broke the stillness.

"I know it's my duty to rescue Gran," she said. "But I keep thinking about my parents…how brave they were… and my grand-mother, too…how do I know I can have courage like theirs? Just days ago I was a tree healer planting seedlings in the forest. Now everyone expects me to be a warrior."

"Maybe it would help you feel more confident if you practiced a little. You bring the branch and we'll go further into the woods. We'll find a place where the trees and bushes are so thick the boggarts won't see us."

Autumn nodded and they slipped away. They found a spot behind a pile of giant boulders. It was dark and silent there, far from watching boggart eyes, but Autumn used her branch to check for boggarts just in case. As soon as they were sure it was safe, the lesson began.

"Now then, raise the branch, focus your attention on that boul-der over there, and blow it up."

Autumn raised the branch. She took a deep breath, aimed, and willed the branch to send a lightning bolt toward the giant rock. But the bolt of light fell far short of its target. Autumn looked up at Lance.

"Try again," he said.

Autumn fired again. But it was still too short. She gritted her teeth and fired three shots in a row. This time two were short, and the third went too far.

"I'll never get this," Autumn said, frustration written all over her face.

"Take it easy," Lance said. He put a reassuring hand on her shoulder. "You've only just started."

She didn't tell him she'd already used the branch to kill a boggart on the beach. After all, killing him had probably been nothing more than luck. She tried again to hit the target, but again she missed. She stood straighter, squinted her eyes, and sent two more lightning bolts toward the rocks. She was getting close, but close wouldn't be enough.

Lance folded his arms across his chest.

"Try again, only this time, pretend the boulder is Azara. Before you fire, think about your parents, remember how they died, then think of your grandmother being helpless in Azara's hands."

Autumn thought back to Forsythia's story of the agonizing way her parents died. She fired once more. This time the boulder exploded into a million burning pieces.

"I knew you could do it," Lance said.

Autumn looked grim. "Maybe, but I don't think I'll ever be a true warrior. The way you killed that boggart at the Council meeting was incredible. I can't even imagine how you did it."

Lance reached down to his boot and pulled out a long, slender blade. "All warriors carry a dagger," he told her. She saw that this one was made of carefully honed black obsidian. He held it out to show it to Autumn. It looked dangerous just lying on his open hand.

"Want me to give you a lesson on how to throw it?" he asked.

"Absolutely!"

"Remember the breakers on the beach?"

"Of course."

"Then picture a wave while you give this a try. First you have to completely relax. Then let the throw begin from the center of your being. Feel it rise upward like a wave as you raise your arm, then crest and break as you snap your hand."

"Show me."

He showed her.

The dagger landed square in the trunk of a nearby tree. Autumn flew to retrieve it.

"Slower this time," she said as she handed it to him.

He did it again.

She brought it back again.

"Do you want to try?"

"Yes."

He handed her the dagger.

"First relax and center yourself. Visualize the motion of a wave as you raise your arm and release the dagger with a snap of your wrist. It's your intent that carries the weapon through to your target. You have to *be* the dagger."

Autumn stood quietly, raised her arm, and threw the dagger. It missed the tree, but not by much.

"Very good," Lance said, obviously pleased with her first attempt. He went to retrieve the dagger.

"Try again."

She went through the entire motion again. This time it stuck squarely in the tree.

"Looks like you're a natural," he said, as he went to retrieve the dagger once more.

Autumn watched him go with a thoughtful expression on her face.

"I want you to know how much I appreciate what you're doing," she said when he returned. "You could have left after you warned the sea elves and returned to the North Woods. Instead you're here, leading us to rescue my grandmother. You're taking a huge risk. Azara may kill us all. I'm very grateful. But I don't understand why you're doing it."

Lance looked quizzical. "Did you expect me to walk away?"

"No, but…"

"It's not every day I have a chance to help rescue the queen of the fairy realm."

"I see," Autumn said.

"Or serve a princess."

Autumn glanced up and her eyes met his. He was smiling, but there was something in his eyes she'd never seen before. She suddenly felt shy as they turned and walked back to camp.

CHAPTER FIFTEEN

It was nearly dawn the next morning. Autumn, Lance, and Dusty crouched behind a clump of grass on the riverbank. They were as close as they could get to the entrance to Dusty's tunnel without being seen by boggart eyes. Captain Bayberry had already left to meet the landing party.

"Where are they?" Dusty whispered, his voice whistling through his big front teeth. "Shouldn't they be here by now?" In his nervousness he kept rubbing his front paws together.

"Don't worry," Lance replied, giving him a reassuring pat on the back. "They'll be here any time now."

"I hope so," Dusty mumbled.

Autumn kept glancing toward the bend in the river, first tightening her hold on the branch, then relaxing her grip when no ship was in sight.

All at once she turned to Dusty. "I know what we need," she told him. "A cup of tea. There's chamomile growing on the ground all around us. You gather a few leaves while I pick a couple of those bluebells over there. They should have just enough dew. I'll warm it with the branch, and we'll both have a wee sip of tea to soothe our nerves."

The two of them did exactly that.

Lance looked amused as he watched them.

"This is the first time I've ever seen anyone have a tea party before a battle," he observed.

Autumn winked at Dusty. "Clearly you've never fought beside a princess," she replied, taking another sip of tea.

"Here they come," Lance whispered a little while later. Three pairs of eyes stared at the river as the bow of the *Wavedancer* came around the bend, with the other two ships in line right behind. Her sails filled as she moved up river toward the entrance to Azara's cave. Dozens of sea elves were already lined up on deck just behind a long row of cannons, with archers lined up behind. The Armada was ready for battle.

Autumn froze. It was time. She grasped the branch so tight her hands hurt.

Across the river Thorn dashed out from behind the rocks. He took aim at the boggart sentry Autumn had spotted earlier on the pile of rocks, and launched a long, lethal porcupine quill with his bow. When the arrow struck, the boggart quivered, screamed, and fell into the river.

The scream alerted other boggarts who suddenly appeared from their encampment on the river bank. They ran to the edge of the river, bows and arrows in hand. The boggart corpse floated in a small eddy at the foot of the cliff, but there was no sign of the enemy who had shot the arrow.

"Good," Lance whispered to Autumn. "Thorn should be well on his way to the woods by now."

But Thorn hadn't gone. Instead of retreating to safety as they'd planned, he'd hidden among the rocks. Suddenly he reappeared, fired a dozen arrows, and disappeared once more. A dozen boggarts fell. In a flash Thorn was back, firing more quills. More boggarts died.

By now a crowd of Azara's soldiers had gathered on the shore. Taking shelter behind the bodies of their dead comrades, they looked for the source of the arrows. It didn't take them long to locate Thorn. The next time he appeared from behind the rocks, an avalanche of arrows flew toward the hedgehog. He dodged most of them, a few glanced off his quills, but one got through and stuck to his side. He tried to fire again, but before he could get off a shot, more boggart arrows flew. This time they clung to his body on every side. He dropped and lay unmoving on the river bank.

Autumn and Lance stared in shock at their fallen companion.

"Oh, Thorn," Autumn whispered, as she clutched her hands together. "Why didn't you flee when you could?"

"We can't stay here!" The gopher exclaimed, snapping them out their distress and pushing them forward. "The ships will be here soon. You've got to rescue your grandmother while Azara is distracted by the sea elves."

Dusty ran to the mound of dirt and pushed it away. Now Autumn and Lance could see the hole that led into the tunnel. Dusty motioned for them to join him.

"Ready?" Lance asked.

"Of course," Autumn replied. But when she faced the opening, a feeling of dread rose up. She hated to enter another dark tunnel after her experience in the mole hole. But if she wanted to rescue her grandmother, she had to dive in.

With her fairy eyes, Autumn could see, though the light from the entrance grew dimmer as she crept along the path. Lance followed close behind. Because the tunnel had been dug by the gopher, there was ample room. Nevertheless Autumn could barely breathe. She longed to turn and run back to the open air behind her, but her grandmother waited below. Autumn didn't pause as she moved through the tunnel that would take them into the cave.

Though Autumn and Lance didn't make a sound as they moved, there was a faint noise echoing in the tunnel. The farther down they went, the louder it got. Eventually Autumn realized she was hearing voices. The closer they were to the cave, the clearer the words became. Autumn recognized her grandmother's voice.

"Just tell me what you want," Autumn heard Rose say.

"That's no way to speak to me," the other voice replied. Autumn and Lance realized at once that the second voice belonged to Azara. "Don't you know I can kill you whenever I want?"

"Yes, you've told me that several times," Rose said. "It's getting boring. Either do it or don't. I'm tired of listening to your threats."

A great flash of light filled the cave. Autumn started to run forward, but Lance pulled her back. "Wait," he whispered in her ear. "If you run in without knowing what you face, she could kill you before you have a chance to rescue anyone."

"Getting rid of you will be a pleasure," they heard Azara say. "I won't need you much longer."

"You might as well kill me now," Rose replied. "If you think the folk of the Fairy Realm will surrender to save my life, you can think again. They will fight you with every ounce of strength they possess. You can forget about ever being queen again."

"You're wrong! My army is greater than those pathetic defenders of the realm."

"You always were a bossy little brat," Rose said, dismissing the former queen of the Fairy Realm as though she were five-years-old.

"I am of royal blood. I deserve respect," Azara said. Her voice got angrier and angrier as Rose refused to be intimidated.

"Respect is something to be earned, and you've never earned it," Rose replied.

"How dare you say that to me? When I was queen, all the folk of the ream obeyed my every command. All but a few insignificant nobodies, that is. And no one paid any attention to them until your precious Marigold came along. Not only did she listen, she believed the wicked things they said. The next thing I knew she and that husband of hers decided to lead a rebellion against me. AGAINST ME! But I showed her!"

"You beast!"

Autumn and Lance heard the chains clang as Rose strained against them.

"I suggest you control yourself," Azara said with a sneer in her voice. "It's only a matter of time until that granddaughter of yours gets here. Then I'll kill you both. My spies tell me she is already on her way. So you see, you're the best bait I could possibly have."

Rose stopped pulling against the chain.

Azara laughed.

Just then the booming sound of ships' cannons reverberated throughout the cave.

"What was that?"Azara cried out. Her voice faded as she raced toward the river entrance.

CHAPTER SIXTEEN

Autumn and Lance raced down the tunnel, anxious to reach Rose as fast as possible now that Azara had left the cave. Suddenly they hit an unexpected slick patch that knocked them both off their feet and sent them sliding out of control. As they slid around a sharp bend, the dim light that had lit their way vanished.

Now the total darkness pressed against them with smothering intensity. Autumn was completely blind, and the suffocating feeling she'd had ever since entering the tunnel threatened to overwhelm her. She reached out nervously, and sighed with relief when her fingers brushed against Lance. He grasped her hand as they slowly moved forward. They soon passed the boulder Dusty had said marked the exit from the tunnel.

Here there was light from the entrance at the other end of the vast cave. Now that they could see again, Lance motioned for Autumn to stay where she was so he could scout out the cave before they stepped fully into view. He quickly disappeared as he made his way along the cave wall.

"They've left two boggarts by the entrance to guard your grand-mother," he told Autumn when he returned. "Everyone else has gone above to fight the sea elves. We need to strike quickly."

"I'll use the branch."

"No, it would attract attention. Leave it to me. I'll get rid of them both without a sound." Once again he flattened himself against the stone wall, and moved along it toward the cave's entrance.

The boggarts were peering out through the exit in an attempt to see what was happening on the river bank. They weren't paying any attention to what was going on inside the cave. To Autumn they just looked like large hulking shadows. But as Lance drew closer, he could see them clearly. One was definitely larger than the other. Lance heard him complaining.

"I ought to be up there. I've killed plenty of fairies in my time. Why should I be stuck down here with that old fool we're holding prisoner? She isn't going anywhere."

"This place gives me the creeps," the other boggart said. "I feel like someone's watching me."

Lance stepped away from the wall. Silently he raised his bow and took aim. Just then the small boggart turned and saw him. Before he could utter a warning, Lance's arrow pierced his heart.

As the first boggart fell, the other turned, reached for his sword. But Lance sent an arrow through him as well. It flew so fast the boggart's sword never left its scabbard. In the space of a heartbeat, both of the evil creatures lay dead on the floor. Lance ran forward to drag the bodies behind a nearby rock, while Autumn ran to her grandmother.

Rose sat on the ground, chained to the cave wall.

"We're here, Gran," Autumn whispered. "We've come to rescue you." She reached out and gently touched her grandmother's cheek. It had only been three days, but somehow Rose looked older to Autumn and awfully tired.

"Are you all right?"

"I am now," her grandmother replied.

"We'll get you out as fast as we can," Lance said joining them.

Lance pulled out his sword and tried to cut the chain that held Rose to the wall, but he couldn't break through the links.

"Here, let me," Autumn said. She carefully pointed the magic branch at the iron ring that held her grandmother. Her grand-mother's eyes widened at the sight of the branch in her granddaugh-ter's hands. A tiny flash of light, and Rose was free.

"Good job!" Lance said. "Now let's go."

"But you only just got here," a voice replied.

Lance and Autumn spun around. Azara stood just inside the entrance to the cave.

Autumn froze as Azara raised her arm. In her hand she held a branch exactly like Autumn's. She pointed it directly at the young fairy. Before Autumn could move, Azara fired. A ball of light crashed into Autumn, knocking her to the ground.

"Leave her alone!" Rose cried out.

At the same time, Lance drew an arrow through his bow, aimed it at Azara, and fired. The arrow exploded in midflight. Azara smiled.

"My point," she said.

"This isn't a game."

"Oh, but it is," Azara responded with a cruel smile. "It's a game of life and death. And I intend to win."

Lance drew his sword and started toward her.

But Autumn had already risen to her feet. She reached out and pulled him back. "I believe this is my fight," she said and held up her branch. Before Azara could fire again, Autumn sent a bolt of lightning flashing toward her. This time it was Azara who was caught by surprise. She winced as the lightning bolt glanced off her shoulder.

"So you dare to take me on," she observed. "Too bad you're no match for me. This isn't even going to last long enough to get interesting."

Azara raised her arm to fire again, but this time Autumn was ready. She sent a powerful fire ball flying across the cave. Azara ducked and then fought back with a lightning bolt of her own. The duel had begun.

At first they tested each other. Azara sent volley after volley. Autumn responded by deflecting her shots, sending them rebounding about the cave. As Autumn's skill increased, so did the speed and strength of Azara's missiles. White hot bolts of energy flew in all directions. Both Autumn and Azara took to the air, the better to dodge each other's blows. Over and over the cave lit up as lightning streaked back and forth. Smoke floated through the cave, and a sound like thunder reverberated from every direction.

Lance and Rose were backed against the wall, with Lance in front to protect Rose from any stray fireballs. Rose looked anxious as she watched the scene before her. Lance kept fingering his sword as if he longed to jump into the fight.

Autumn's confidence grew now that the battle was on. Totally focused, she aimed every shot with an iron control. Azara's shots grew more frenzied as she dodged Autumn's blows and then fired her own.

The next time Azara aimed a fire ball, Autumn ducked. When it had passed by, she advanced toward Azara.

"Surrender!" she commanded.

"You little fool, you can't defeat me."

With renewed purpose, Azara aimed dozens of white hot balls of fire at Autumn, who blocked each one with a blazing bolt of her own. Back and forth, the lightning flashed. Autumn's face was tight with concentration. Azara's face betrayed her frustration. She hadn't expected Autumn to fight the way she did.

Neither of the two combatants could gain an advantage. But neither of them showed any sign of giving in either.

A wounded boggart staggered into the cave from the direction of the river, an arrow sticking out of his back.

"Help us, Your Majesty," he gasped as he fell to the ground. But Azara ignored him as she kept her attention on Autumn.

Another boggart entered the cave. This one didn't make a sound. It took on the color of the cave wall, and was nearly invisible as it glided to a place just behind Autumn. Lance only spotted it out of the corner of his eye when it drew its sword, preparing to stab Autumn in the back.

"Oh no, you don't!" Lance raised his bow. An arrow instantly pierced the boggart's heart. It was dead before its body hit the floor. Lance remained on guard, his bow and arrows ready, watching for anything else that threatened Autumn.

With both Autumn and Azara exerting all their power to defeat the other, the watchers began to wonder when the battle would end. Bolts of fire continually ricocheted around the cave, one moment near the roof, the next on the floor. Between the gathering smoke, and the repeated flashes of light in the darkness, it was hard for Lance and Rose to see where the bolts came from and where they went.

Autumn's strength grew with every blow. She began to move ever closer to her enemy.

"That's for my mother," she said aiming a blast at Azara, "And that's for my father." The pair of blows, aimed at Azara's head, forced her to veer to the side.

Autumn advanced with cold fury. Recognizing Autumn's power, Azara gathered all of her own strength to respond. She took aim and sent a white hot beam surging directly at Autumn's heart. Autumn saw it coming and raised her arm to block its fire. It struck with greater force than any previous lightning bolt, a direct hit that scorched her arm, knocked her to the ground, and ignited her magic branch.

The burning branch dropped from her hand as Autumn fell to her knees, and then slumped to the cave's cold stone floor. She lay there without moving. The watchers were stunned, while Azara gloated in triumph. With an exultant look aimed at Lance, she said "As you see, it was a game after all. And I won." She laughed, savoring her victory.

But Lance didn't hear. All his attention was focused on Autumn. His whole body tensed as he leaned forward, looking for a sign of life. He was ready to rush to her, but something told him to stay back. As he watched, he saw a faint intake of breath. She was injured, but she was alive.

"What a failure you are," Azara said to the silent fairy lying on the floor of the cave. "You're as feeble as your parents, another easy victim of my power."

The blow had knocked her out, but Autumn's consciousness was returning. Her determination to destroy Azara filled her body like a surging tide. When she heard Azara's words they lit a blaze of anger inside her.

She opened her eyes and without moving, glanced around the area where she lay. Just inches away she saw the body of the boggart Lance had killed. She wondered if boggarts carried daggers like elf warriors. She spotted a glint of metal at the rim of his boot. *Yes!*

Meanwhile a gloating Azara approached her defeated adversary. Just as she was about to aim a final blast, an enraged Rose stepped forward.

"You killed my daughter. Now you've killed my grandchild! You won't get away with this. I'll fight you myself!" With her fists clenched she looked ready to pull Azara apart with her bare hands.

Azara turned away from Autumn, and with an evil smile, aimed her branch at Rose.

"Oh no you don't!" Autumn's cry echoed throughout the cave.

Faster than a frog's tongue, Autumn rose up and lunged for the dagger. In one smooth motion she pulled it from the boggart's boot, raised her arm, and threw with all her might.

The dagger pierced Azara's arm, causing her to drop her magic branch to the floor of the cave. She screamed and clutched her wounded arm as Autumn dove to retrieve the fallen branch.

"Surrender!" Autumn demanded, as she picked up Azara's branch and aimed it at her enemy. "You're finished. It's over. You're defeated again."

"I think not," Azara replied. She held her wounded arm against her body. "You may have won this battle, but I will win the war."

She spun around and flew toward the tunnel that led to the woods. Autumn had just raised the branch to take aim and stop her when they heard loud voices and running feet coming toward them down that same tunnel.

"The snake is coming! Run for your lives!"

Captain Bayberry and the sea elves from the Armada burst into view.

"Stop!" he shouted, when he saw Azara flying toward him. "Don't go that way!"

"Do you take me for a fool? I'm not going to fall for an old trick like that!"

Azara shot up over the sea elves, and flew into the tunnel.

"Halt!" Captain Bayberry shouted again. But Azara had already disappeared. Seconds later a scream of terror echoed throughout the cave. The scream was abruptly cut off.

"Let's get out of here!" Lance shouted. He gathered Autumn into his arms and raced for Dusty's tunnel. Captain Bayberry picked Rose up and followed with the sea elves right behind.

CHAPTER SEVENTEEN

When Autumn and the others emerged from the tunnel, they saw the *Wavedancer* just offshore. Bodies of Azara's boggarts were scattered everywhere; there wasn't a living boggart in sight.

Lance set Autumn down on the riverbank.

"I could have flown on my own," she told him, though she was suffering intense pain from the burn left by Azara's final blow.

"Of course you could," he replied. In spite of the pain, her face relaxed into a small smile. She turned to Dusty who waited nearby.

"Thank you," she said. "We never could have done this without you. You are definitely the bravest gopher I've ever met."

"It's been a pleasure," he replied, his words whistling through his two front teeth as they always did. "Now if you don't mind I'll get out of here. I don't want to find out if that snake follows you up the tunnel."

With that the furry creature turned and scurried toward the woods.

"We'd better go too," Lance said.

They hurried to the shore where a group of sea elves waited with Captain Marina's longboat to take them out to the ship. Autumn and her grandmother sat in the bow of the boat, with Lance and Captain Bayberry right behind them, as the other sea elves climbed on board.

While the boat made its way onto the river, Rose took Azara's branch from Autumn and moved it across the young fairy's body. Autumn felt velvety warmth, like melted chocolate, flow through her. The pain lessened.

"Thank you, Gran," Autumn said with a sigh. "You always know how to make things better."

"My dear child, it's you who has made things better. You're the one who has finally defeated Azara. It took great courage to fight as you did. You reminded me of your mother."

"Oh Gran, I'm not like her at all. I'm just a tree healer who learned to fight so I could save you," Autumn said. "My mother was a great warrior."

"No, dear," Rose replied. "Your mother was a teacher. She only learned to fight because the folk of the realm begged her to free them from Azara. And your father was the same. Hawk was a ranger. He spent his time working to preserve the forests. He became an elf warrior so he could fight beside your mother and save the folk of the Realm. And you are just like them. Not only do you share their courage, but you have their compassion as well."

Autumn was confused. She'd always believed her parents were highly trained warriors. Now it seemed they were just fairy folk like she was. Her mother had been part of the royal family, it was true, but she hadn't been in line for the throne until Azara was banished without heirs of her own. Marigold had never wanted to be queen.

Just then the longboat arrived beside the *Wavedancer*. The sea elves helped Rose climb the ladder to the deck. But for Autumn, Lance and Captain Bayberry, the job wasn't finished. They had to find Thorn's body. They owed him that.

Half a dozen sea elves rowed them to the other bank. As soon as they landed, they began to search for the little hedgehog. They found him at the edge of the woods where he had managed to crawl after he was hit.

Autumn and Lance stood and gazed down at their fallen comrade. It was quiet on the riverbank now that the noise of the battle was over. Thorn lay still on the ground, his body slightly rounded as if trying to protect himself from further harm, his front paws curled up against his chest. He might have been asleep except for the dozens of long dark quills, three times as long as his own, which stuck out from every part of his body.

"Poor Thorn," Autumn whispered as tears gathered in her eyes. "Look at all those arrows. I hate to think of how he must have suffered." The tears spilled over.

"He was as brave as any soldier I've known," Lance said. "I couldn't believe the way he kept coming back, over and over, even after he was hit."

As the other elves approached in silence, bearing a cloth to wrap around the body, Lance knelt down beside the little hedgehog. He gazed at Thorn's body for a long moment a tiny frown between his eyes. He reached out and put a hand on Thorn's chest. Suddenly he gave a great shout. "He's alive!"

"What?" Autumn dropped down beside Lance.

"The branch, Autumn, use the branch. Maybe you can save him."

Autumn reached out and began to move the branch back and forth across the hedgehog's body,

"Come back, Thorn," she repeated over and over. "Let the branch heal you. Please come back to us."

The hedgehog lay without moving, but Autumn could see his breathing grow stronger. Back and forth she passed the branch. At last he opened his eyes. He blinked at the faces gathered around him as they all sighed with relief.

A closer inspection revealed that many of the arrows had gotten tangled in his protective coat of quills before they reached his flesh. Others had penetrated to his body, but only one had delivered what could have become a fatal wound.

"Oh Thorn, what a fright you gave us," Autumn said as she reached out to gently stroke the top of his head. "You're a hero, you know. You killed more than a dozen boggarts all by yourself. You lured them all out of the cave before the *Wavedancer* even arrived."

The young hedgehog's eyes focused on Autumn. "Could you tell Peony?" he asked.

"Of course," Autumn replied.

He gave a satisfied sigh, then closed his eyes and sank into an exhausted slumber.

"I'll stay with him until his family gets here," Captain Bayberry told Autumn and Lance. "We can dispatch a messenger bird to tell them where he is."

"Make sure the bird tells them to bring Peony," Autumn said with a smile.

She leaned forward and kissed Thorn's little black nose. Then she and Lance stood and headed back to the longboat.

Once on board the *Wavedancer,* Lance and Autumn walked to the stern where they stood and looked at the scene of the battle.

"It's funny," Autumn said. "I keep thinking about my parents. I feel closer to them now than I ever have before. I suppose it's because I've learned so much more about them."

"Maybe it's also because when you defeated Azara you accomplished what they set out to do."

"I didn't exactly intend for it to end the way it did."

"That doesn't matter. You fought and you won. You used the skill of a true warrior to take away her branch. Even if it was the snake that finally killed her, it was because of you that she fled up the tunnel."

"Maybe, but I couldn't have done any of it without *you*. After all, you taught me to throw a dagger, and you killed the boggart that would have stabbed me in the back."

He shook his head. "That's all very well, your Highness, but it was you that defeated Azara. It's important that you, and everyone else, understand that."

She smiled slightly. "So we all know that I have what it takes to be queen?"

He nodded. "That's right."

Her expression grew serious as her gaze met his. "You're right. I guess I have learned to be a warrior. But I've also learned how important it is to have loyal companions. Not only did you make a difference, but Thorn, Dahlia, Dusty, and the sea elves were all part of our victory as well. And then there was the branch from the golden tree…

"When I first accepted the branch, I planned to return it as soon as possible. I was afraid of its power, afraid I might be tempted to use it for the wrong reasons. Yet when I fought Azara, even knowing she'd killed my parents, I couldn't take her life. At the end, I was trying to keep her from escaping, not kill her. So I think I'll keep the branch. I want to use it for good to make up for the way Azara used it for evil. I think that would please the golden tree."

Lance looked as if he had something to say but wasn't sure how to say it.

"I realize there is danger in possessing such power," Autumn said, guessing what was on his mind. "That's why I need someone I can trust at my side. So I wonder…would you be my chief advisor when I am queen?" Her words were confident, but the look she gave him was uncertain.

He didn't hesitate. "It would be an honor."

She reached out, shook his hand to seal the deal, and smiled. He smiled in return, and then kept her hand in his as they went below to join the victory celebration.